VICTORIAN
MANSION
FLOWER SHOP
MYSTERIES™

Weeds of Doubt

Sandra Orchard

Annie's®
AnniesFiction.com

Books in the Victorian Mansion Flower Shop Mysteries series

Library of Congress-in-Publication Data
Weeds of Doubt / by Sandra Orchard
p. cm.
I. Title
                              2018958650

AnniesFiction.com
(800) 282-6643
Victorian Mansion Flower Shop Mysteries™
Series Creators: Shari Lohner, Janice Tate
Editor: Jane Haertel
Cover Illustrator: Bob Kayganich

10 11 12 13 14 | Printed in China | 9 8 7 6 5 4

1

DeeDee Wilcox burst into the Old Cape Lighthouse keeper's quarters, her sun-streaked blonde hair bouncing around her shoulders, her cheeks flushed. "We desperately need your help," she said to the rest of the Petal Pushers garden club, who had assembled for their biweekly meeting. The second part of "we" trailed DeeDee through the door, uncertainty written on her face.

"Of course we'll help if we can." Kaylee Bleu glanced from Jessica Roberts, who was setting out the chocolate treats she'd brought from her bakery, to Mary Bishop, who was sitting on the sofa. "Right, girls?"

Mary—who at sixty, didn't fit the "girls" moniker any more than Jessica, who was tickling fifty—grinned. "Absolutely! And we always love to welcome visitors too," she said to DeeDee's friend.

"Sorry." DeeDee motioned to the petite, dark-haired woman standing behind her. "This is Wilma Graham. She's been organizing a high school reunion."

"For your class?" Kaylee asked.

"No, I was a couple of years behind her in school, but it's more than that. She's the school librarian and she's been working on creating an Alumni Hall of Fame too. The plan had been to unveil it all for their twenty-five-year reunion, but we just learned our school's most beloved teacher and coach has been having some serious health concerns. He's put his house up for sale and plans to move out east to be closer to his family. And you know how quickly houses sell in the summer months here."

Jessica nodded. "My neighbor's sold in forty-eight hours."

"Exactly," DeeDee said. "We've decided to schedule the reunion for the last weekend of August. Labor Day is that Monday, so we'll be able to extend activities right through Sunday and still give everyone a day to travel home before the new workweek."

Kaylee counted quickly on her phone's calendar app. "That's only four weeks away."

"That's why we need help," Wilma said. Her voice was quiet and shy. "Alumni need to be contacted. Venues need to be booked. Activities planned. Accommodations secured." Tears sprang to her eyes and she shook her head. "I don't know if it's even possible, but I know everyone would want Mr. Fletcher to be at the reunion. He was the best teacher ever. He helped so many kids, and we were his last class. He retired the year we graduated."

DeeDee squeezed her hand. "If anyone can do it, the Petal Pushers can."

"Accommodations shouldn't be too big a deal," Kaylee said. "I don't have any weddings scheduled that weekend, and if there was one, I would have at least heard about it, so the Turtle Cove Inn shouldn't be clogged with wedding guests."

"Besides," Jessica added, "a lot of the alumni traveling in from off island would probably have family or friends still here they could stay with. But I know the manager of the Turtle Cove Inn. I can talk to him about reserving a block of rooms for a group rate. And I'd be happy to help with food." Jessica held up a plate of flower-shaped chocolates, her eyes twinkling.

"Ooh." DeeDee reached for a chocolate sunflower on a stick. "These are gorgeous."

"If you didn't already have a theme in mind," Mary chimed in, "we could make it flower-related. We are the Petal Pushers after all."

"That's actually a great idea." Wilma beamed. "Our high school prom had a flower theme, and Mr. Fletcher used to help organize the poinsettia fund-raiser every year at Christmastime."

Kaylee frowned. "Well, I'm not sure how many poinsettias I could get in for an August event, but I can try. And Mary and I can take care of decorating whatever venues you decide on."

"And help brainstorm activity ideas?" DeeDee pressed.

"Our brains are at your disposal," Kaylee replied with a grin. The women laughed.

"This is so great." Wilma plopped into the closest empty chair and pulled a thick binder from her book bag. "I'll show you what ideas I've already compiled."

Three hours later, when the sun had slipped into the ocean, painting the sky and water brilliant colors, the Petal Pushers left the lighthouse keeper's quarters, each armed with a page full of duties to complete by the next meeting.

The month to the reunion had flown by and Kaylee scrambled to put the finishing touches to her share of the preparations. She finished taping a *Welcome Turtle Cove Alumni* banner to the front window of her flower shop, The Flower Patch, and stepped back to examine the result.

Reese Holt came out of Jessica's bakery next door with a cup of coffee and stopped at Kaylee's side. "Looks good."

Bear, Kaylee's lovable dachshund, danced excitedly around his legs. Reese was one of the dog's favorite people on earth, besides Kaylee.

Reese stooped and greeted the little dachshund. "When's this whole shindig set to start?" he asked Kaylee.

Kaylee glanced at her watch and felt her heart rate tick up. "Any minute! And I still have three more venues to finish decorating."

"I can give you a hand."

"No, that's okay. I'm sure you have a job to get back to." With Reese's stellar reputation as a master carpenter and all-around handyman, everyone in town always seemed to be trying to schedule his services.

"I'm ahead of schedule at the moment. And I'd be happy to help. I may not be an alumnus of Turtle Cove High, but I know Mr. Fletcher and I think it's great that Wilma wanted to pull this together before he moved away."

"Thanks. I really appreciate it. You could start by loading the arrangements by the door into the van." She turned to Mary, who worked part-time at The Flower Patch. They went inside the shop. "We're stop number three on DeeDee's Turtle Cove Crawl this afternoon, so I should be back to give you a hand before too many alumni show up."

Mary dismissed her with a wave. "I can handle it. I've got the clues right here to help them figure out their next destination."

"Do you mind if I leave Bear with you?"

"I never do."

"Thanks." She grabbed a box to take to the van, then paused. "When the photographer gets here, he can take the formal shots of each alumni under the arbor or—wait, do you think the lighting in here is bright enough? But a professional would come prepared with his or her own, right?"

"Go," Mary ordered. "I'll take care of the photographer."

"Thanks!" Kaylee dashed out behind Reese, carrying the last load of sunflowers to the van.

"Where to first?" Reese asked, climbing into the passenger's seat.

"Get Wired," Kaylee said. "We chose places that used to be popular hangouts back in the day."

Reese laughed. "That explains why Keith had the old computers and video games on display. Get Wired was probably the closest thing Turtle Cove had to a video arcade."

"That's what Wilma said. And I'm sure the guys won't notice much else there, so we figured we'd need an eye-catching clue to get their attention away from the video games."

Kaylee parked at the curb in front of the electronics store. "The sunflowers?"

"Yup." Kaylee jumped down from the van and grabbed one of the large pots.

Reese picked up the other and then hurried ahead to open the shop door. "I don't get it. Where does a sunflower tell them to go next? Are you counting on the flowers turning toward the light, which also happens to be the direction of the next location?"

"That would have required some serious planning. And to be honest, I didn't even think of it. What do you get from sunflowers?"

His brow furrowed. "Seeds and oil. Oh! So from here they're supposed to go to the health food store?"

"That's right." Kaylee set her sunflower on one side of the vintage video game display Keith had set up and then shifted Reese's pot into place on the other side.

"But I thought the destinations were supposed to be places where the alumni hung out during high school? I find it hard to believe the health food store was all that popular."

Kaylee laughed. "It probably wouldn't have been if it'd been here. But back in the day, that place was a music store, very popular with rock star wannabes, according to DeeDee." Kaylee drove them to the next location she needed to decorate. "Not all the destinations were hangouts either. Some, like DeeDee's shop, are businesses that belong to alumni from different years."

"So how does The Flower Patch fit?" Reese asked. "Is it grandfathered in because your dad and grandparents went to Turtle Cove High?"

Kaylee grinned. "No, it was the most popular place for the

guys to buy the corsages for their prom dates."

"So the corsages are a clue for your store? Here I thought it would be for the high school gym or wherever they held the prom."

"I imagine Wilma hopes you won't be the only one who makes that mistake. We didn't want to make it too easy." Kaylee and Reese made short work of finishing setup at the remaining venues. Her cell phone rang as she parked once more outside The Flower Patch. She glanced at the caller ID—DeeDee.

DeeDee was already standing on the sidewalk in front, her phone pressed to her ear, and when she spotted the van, she clicked off her phone and dashed toward Kaylee, her face frantic. "The photographer bailed on us. What are we going to do? Wilma's counting on those photos for the special collage she has planned for Mr. Fletcher."

Reese rounded the van. "Why don't you ask Arnold Boyer?"

"The dentist? You know him? I thought he left the island long before you arrived."

"We met in college. He's here for the reunion. I saw him at the coffee shop an hour ago." Reese pulled out his phone and tapped the screen. "He gave me his number. He used to be a photographer for the college yearbook."

"Yeah, I think he took pictures for Turtle Cove High's yearbook too," DeeDee said.

"See?" Reese said, listening to his phone ring. "I'm sure he'll be happy to fill in for your photographer."

"You think he has a decent camera with him? I think Wilma was hoping for better pictures than could be taken on a phone."

"His girlfriend had a fancy DSLR camera hanging around her neck."

"Perfect!" DeeDee squealed.

Wilma, who'd walked up behind DeeDee, didn't seem nearly as thrilled about the option.

"I know you wanted a photographer who wasn't part of the group," Kaylee said to her. "But if you want his girlfriend in some of the pictures, one of us could take a few with her in them."

Wilma shook her head. "Don't worry about it. She's not one of our classmates, and this weekend is mostly for them."

Reese pocketed his phone. "Sounds as if Arnold's girl, Amber Mason, is already on the job. He says they've got a whole gang at the park reenacting some of his old yearbook photos."

"Yes," Wilma said softly, "I'd e-mailed him that I hoped to do that."

A swell of hoots and hollers came from the direction of the park.

DeeDee beelined toward it. "This I've got to see!"

"Sounds like they're having fun," Kaylee said encouragingly to Wilma, who looked gloomier than ever.

"Let's see what they're up to," Reese suggested, nudging them both toward the laughter.

The park came into view and Reese burst into laughter. "This is not going to end well."

People of all shapes and sizes were on their hands and knees forming a pyramid. The petite woman on the second row didn't appear nearly strong enough to hold the solidly built man being helped up onto her back, but she was clearly giving it her best effort.

A redheaded bombshell stood behind them shaking her head. "There's no way I'm standing on the top."

Kaylee gasped. "Is that Ginger Andrews? The soap opera queen?"

"Yup. She's Turtle Cove's claim to fame," Wilma said.

A tall, dapper gentleman, whose stylish salt-and-pepper hair and square-cut chin could have easily landed him a role as her leading man, whispered something in her ear. He must have paid her quite a compliment from the way she blushed.

"Who's the guy talking to her?" Kaylee asked.

"Reggie Blake. He was our prom king. Now he's an electronics magnate."

"And let me guess," Reese interjected. "Ginger was the prom queen?"

"No, that was actually his wife, Nina, but she couldn't make it to the reunion."

Whatever Reggie said to Ginger convinced her to let him help her to the top of the pyramid. As she stepped up the second row, the whole thing began to wobble.

Kaylee covered her face. "I can't watch." But she peeked between her fingers.

As Ginger stepped to the pinnacle and spread her arms in a victory V, the whole pyramid collapsed like a house of cards. A muscled young man dashed into the fray just in time to catch Ginger before she hit the ground—not that his heroic catch stopped her shrill scream. Everyone within earshot who hadn't already been watching came running, cell phones out as they took videos and pictures. And Ginger clearly wasn't happy about being caught in such a pose. She glared all around as the giggling group behind her untangled themselves.

"I'm guessing that doesn't match the photo in the yearbook," Kaylee said to Wilma.

She giggled. "Actually, it's pretty close."

Reese waved over a slight, dark-haired man wearing round, black-rimmed glasses. "This is Arnold," he said, then introduced Kaylee.

Somehow the man looked like a dentist. He was at least half a foot shorter than Reese, clean-shaven and handsome in a different way from Reese's rugged attractiveness. But from the dreamy expression Kaylee caught on Wilma's face, she definitely preferred Arnold's type.

Arnold glanced around the crowd, trying to find his girlfriend, Amber. "She's the redhead," he said, standing on his tiptoes to scan the park grounds. "Not Ginger, but every bit as beautiful."

Wilma frowned. "We'd better encourage everyone to get started on the crawl or some of the businesses will be ready to close before everyone does the rounds."

"There she is," Arnold pointed to a redhead slinking into the bushes next to the trailhead, snapping photos of couples strolling along the trail.

"Oh no!" Kaylee ran toward her with Arnold, Reese, and Wilma on her heels. "Excuse me, Miss. You don't want to be in there. That tall plant with the white, plate-sized flowers is *Heracleum mantegazzianum*."

Amber's forehead wrinkled.

"Giant hogweed. It's poisonous." Kaylee pointed to the posted warning sign.

Amber's expression transformed to one of panic. She pulled her arms tight to her body and dashed into the clearing. "Thanks for telling me!"

Ginger stepped onto the trail and squinted in their direction. The rugged young man who'd saved her when the pyramid collapsed trailed a few feet behind her, and from the way he scanned the area every few seconds, Kaylee guessed that he was the actress's bodyguard. Ginger stomped over to Amber, her hands fisted at her side. "Who are you?"

Amber straightened, clearly not happy with Ginger's tone.

"She's my date," Arnold said protectively.

Ginger turned on him. "Well, I'm here to relax with old friends, not be hounded by the paparazzi, so make sure your girlfriend doesn't leak any pictures to the papers, or you'll both be sorry."

Reggie slipped into their midst and laid a soothing hand on

her arm. "Of course they wouldn't do that." He gazed pointedly at Amber. "Would you?"

Amber's defiant countenance didn't make any promises.

"Amber volunteered to fill in when our photographer bailed," Wilma interjected. "We're lucky to have her."

Ginger snorted.

"Ginger, why don't we get started on this town crawl? The less time you spend in a given place, the less likely someone is to catch a photo of you and leak it," Reggie coaxed.

The actress hesitated for a moment, then nodded, and the pair strolled off.

Arnold's expression turned wistful. "He still has the magic touch." A hint of envy colored his tone. "He was always the most popular guy in school."

"Maybe to airheads like Ginger," Wilma muttered. More audibly, she said, "He always seemed a little phony to me."

"You should go back to your hotel and wash with soap and water to make sure there's no hogweed sap on you," Kaylee advised Amber, "and change your clothes to be on the safe side. I'd recommend long sleeves and pants for the next several days. If your skin came into contact with the plant and is then exposed to sunlight, you'll get some nasty blistering burns. Some people have even been hospitalized from their exposure to that plant."

"I'm sorry. I know you need me taking pictures at The Flower Patch," Amber said to Wilma. "I won't be long, I promise." She lifted her camera from around her neck and handed it to Arnold. "You get started and I'll catch up to you at the flower shop."

"I should walk you back to the hotel," Arnold countered.

"No," Amber insisted. "I don't want you to miss out on a moment of your reunion because I was too busy taking pictures to read a sign. Kaylee, do you think I'll be okay?"

"I'm sure you'll be fine if you wash right away," Kaylee reassured her. "I think I'll have a word with the town about cordoning off this area to make sure no one walks into the plant again."

"Why doesn't the town get rid of them?" Wilma asked as Amber left.

"They are trying to," Kaylee explained, "but it will take several years to get rid of a mature plant like this. It's been here probably five years or so, and it's been dropping seeds into the surrounding soil all that time. If they pull it while it has seeds, they risk spreading it. And even if they pull this plant, the seeds already planted can live for up to five years, so it'll simply keep growing. The best thing to do is spray it with an herbicide during its growing season to prevent it creating more seeds and continue to do so until it uses up the stockpile of seeds already in the soil."

"Well they'd better do something before someone gets seriously hurt."

2

Around five o'clock, Kaylee began bringing in the sidewalk displays she'd set out for the Turtle Cove Crawl.

A balding man waved at her from across the street. "Excuse me. I need to talk to you." He hurried over, hampered by a slight limp and followed by a blonde with thick glasses that slipped down her nose.

Arnold and Amber emerged from Jessica's shop next door, and Amber brought up her ever-present camera and snapped a few pictures.

The blonde woman paused at the display of DeeDee's handcrafted soaps as the man addressed Kaylee. "You're the owner, right?"

"That's right."

"Then you must know a lot about plants."

"A fair amount, yes."

"Good." He pulled a yellow card from his pocket that Kaylee recognized as one of the clue cards for the town crawl. "What's a popular Chinese maple used in bonsai gardens that would have made King Neptune proud?"

Kaylee smiled, impressed by the clever clue Wilma had devised. "Do you know what King Neptune is usually depicted holding?" Kaylee asked.

The man glanced back at his wife. "Cheryl, do you?"

The woman set down a bar of soap and ambled closer. "Yes, a trident. Is there such a thing as a trident maple?"

"There is. The *Acer buergerianum*."

The man studied a map of the town. "I don't see any businesses called trident. Is it this Gumshoe Place? Trident is a brand of chewing gum, right?"

Arnold shared a smile with Kaylee over their heads as the man's wife glanced at the map. "You need to put on your reading glasses. That says Gunther's Sea Kayak rentals."

Arnold sidled up to Cheryl and whispered, "The Latin name Miss Bleu gave you was another hint."

"It was?" Cheryl's eyes widened and her gaze shifted back to Kaylee. "What did you say it was again?"

"*Acer buergerianum.*"

"Buergerianium? It's got to be the burger joint," the man said. "Although the pronunciation is a little different. Isn't that where you said you always hung out on Friday nights with your classmates?"

The woman peered at Kaylee for confirmation.

Kaylee feigned an "I'm not supposed to say" shrug that reassured them they were on the right track.

The woman grinned. "Thanks!"

Amber snapped a picture of the pair.

Cheryl frowned at her. "Do I know you?"

Arnold introduced her as his date, and Cheryl introduced her husband, Phil Newton.

"We were charged with capturing a portrait of every alumni in attendance," Arnold explained. "We had a display set up inside the flower shop."

"And I remember seeing you collecting a clue at the counter inside this afternoon," Amber interjected. "But I think we missed getting a formal photo. I think we could do with more candid shots anyway, though."

"Fine by me, as long as you get my good side." Cheryl laughed and fell into reminiscing about school days with Arnold while Kaylee returned to closing up the shop.

"I'll take care of putting those away," Mary said when Kaylee carried the last display in from the sidewalk. "You need to hurry home and freshen up for your date."

"It isn't a date. Reese just asked me if I'd come along to the reunion dinner so he wouldn't be the only non-alumni there. Arnold talked him into going."

Mary shook her head and said to Bear, "What are we going to do with her?"

Kaylee rolled her eyes and scooped her dachshund into her arms. "The last thing I want to do is sabotage our friendship by reading more into a dinner invitation than there is."

"Whatever you say. Oh, and a last-minute order came in to be delivered to the soap opera star at her hotel first thing tomorrow morning. I put it together and stored it in the first cooler. Will you be able to deliver it?"

"Sure. No problem. I'll see you tomorrow."

By the time Kaylee arrived at the Pacific Street Diner an hour later, the place was packed. The usual top-forty playlist had been replaced with tunes from those of the alumni's high school days, but Ginger and Reggie were the only ones dancing on the small dance floor. Across the room, Reese waved from his table.

After pulling her chair out for her, he made introductions. "You already know Amber and Arnold and Wilma." He motioned to the man next to Wilma. "This is Ewan Sutherland."

Ewan stood and reached across the table to shake Kaylee's hand. He might have been another soap opera star—tall, dark, and handsome—but Reese said he was a veterinarian, living off the island. "You're the flower shop owner with the little dachshund, aren't you?" he asked.

"That's right."

The last couple at the table introduced themselves. They turned out to be Phil and Cheryl Newton, the pair she'd helped with the trident maple clue.

Arnold was watching Reggie and Ginger on the dance floor. "I wish I could dance like that. I swear there's nothing the man can't do."

Phil glanced over his shoulder and snorted. "Trust me. You're a much better man than he is."

"That's what I always tried to tell him," Wilma said.

"How do you know him?" Kaylee asked Phil. "I got the impression earlier that you didn't grow up in Turtle Cove."

Phil downed the last of his soda before responding. "You're right. I didn't. I met Cheryl and Reggie at college. Then after college we went into business together."

"It didn't work out, I take it?" Amber asked.

Phil twirled his glass, watching the ice swirl. "Actually we did great. But after a while our visions for the company headed in different directions, so we split."

"And you went to work for someone else?" Amber asked.

"No, no. Cheryl and I started our own company and he still has the old one."

"What kind of business?" Reese asked.

"The tech industry."

His wife must have seen Wilma's and Ewan's eyes glaze over, because she patted her husband's hand. "Enough about us. What do you do for a living, Amber?"

"Please don't shush him. I think it's great when people are brave enough to strike out on their own and become entrepreneurs. And you've done it twice?" Amber directed that last comment back to Phil.

"Yes." He folded his wife's hands in his. "But I recently retired from the business so we could enjoy our health while we have it. There's more to life than making money."

"Wow," Arnold said. "You've done well for yourself to retire so young. I figure I'll have to work until I'm sixty at least. Longer if I get married and start a family."

Wilma rubbed her thumbnail along a groove in the wooden table. "Would you like to start a family?"

He glanced at Amber, whose attention had shifted to photographing the growing group on the dance floor. "Sure, if I find the right woman."

The color that rushed to Wilma's cheeks told Kaylee plainly that Wilma wished she were that woman.

"How about you two?" Ewan asked Phil and Cheryl. "You have kids?"

"No, we never did," Cheryl said. "We tried for a few years, but it never happened. I enjoy working though."

"You didn't retire when your husband did?" Amber interjected. Obviously she hadn't been paying attention to the conversation.

Cheryl's eyes narrowed as if she resented the question. "No. Like I said, I enjoy my work."

"Are you involved in research and development?"

"I mostly crunch numbers."

"Cheryl was always a whiz at math in school," Wilma chimed in.

"And I guess having Phil at home helps lighten the load of household chores?" Ewan said, with a twinkle in his eye.

Cheryl smiled. "Yes."

"I'm thinking of taking a gourmet cooking course," Phil added. "To give her extra-special treats to come home to."

"What a sweet idea," Wilma cooed.

"You never did tell us what you do, Amber," Cheryl said.

"Nothing terribly exciting. Just office work."

Ewan laughed. "On the days when I have cats trying to shred my arms or a dog trying to make a meal of a finger, I sometimes wish my job could be so unexciting." He winked at her, earning a giggle.

The alumni of the table soon became immersed in regaling each other with stories from high school, while Amber wandered off to take photos of the groups at the other tables.

Kaylee turned to Reese. "How serious do you think Amber and Arnold are?" she whispered.

"I'm under the impression they've only known each other a couple of weeks," Reese said.

Kaylee stifled a grimace. If Arnold was inviting her to his class reunion after a mere two-week acquaintance, it must be pretty serious, at least on his part. Poor Wilma didn't have a chance.

Amber scurried back to the table and tapped Wilma's shoulder. "I have a fabulous idea. So many people are snapping photos with their cell phones. You should invite them to send all their photos to you and you could post them on a private social media group so everyone can enjoy them and download copies of ones they'd like to keep. I could set it up for you, if you like. We could even make a slide show of them for the final night or to play during the dinner dance. That way, everyone can enjoy all the photos, not only the ones I take."

"That *is* a fabulous idea!" Wilma stood right up and made the announcement, sharing the e-mail address she'd created for the reunion.

Kaylee ordered a burger and fries and, while she ate, enjoyed listening to everyone's stories. Amber seemed to spend more time away from the table than at it, even sharing a dance with Arnold's idol, Reggie, which gave Kaylee a smidgen of optimism that there might be hope for a match between Wilma and Arnold yet.

"This doesn't look good," Reese said out of the blue.

Kaylee followed his gaze to see an attractive blonde woman in tight jeans, three-inch heels, and a shimmery, clingy top stalking toward Reggie and Ginger on the dance floor. "Who's that?"

Cheryl twisted around in her chair. "Uh-oh. That's Nina, Reggie's wife. Someone said she was recovering from plastic surgery at a European spa and that's why he was here without her."

"People can be so cruel," Kaylee said. "You'd think by this age they'd be too mature for all that high school cattiness."

"No, it's true," Wilma said. "At least, the part about Reggie coming alone. Nina isn't registered for the reunion."

As Nina made her way to Ginger and Reggie, the pale fury on her face transformed into a placid mask. She tapped Ginger on the shoulder and apparently asked to cut in, because Ginger stepped back and Nina moved into her husband's arms, although he didn't seem particularly pleased to see her.

Reggie escorted Nina to his table before the song finished. Thankfully, Ginger and her apparent bodyguard had already relocated to a pair of stools at the bar, sparing them from an uncomfortable situation.

Nina summoned the waitress a little too loudly and ordered herself a glass of wine against her husband's wishes, so she changed it to a martini, clearly to spite him.

"Did they always have such a rocky relationship?" Amber asked Cheryl.

"Nina grew up spoiled and beautiful. Of course, Reggie could afford to dote on her. But he's also a horrible flirt. He really does adore her, but she started to lose her self-confidence and took to drinking too much, which he never liked."

"When we were business partners," Phil interjected, "we maintained a strict two-drink limit for any public event. Business owners can't afford to jeopardize the integrity of their company by having a few too many and having their judgment impaired, you know?"

Ewan, the vet sitting beside Wilma, who'd been quietly watching the comings and goings most of the evening, said, "Seems like Reggie has his hands full trying to ensure Nina follows suit."

"Enough of this gloomy talk," Amber said brightly. "As a whole your classmates seem to be quite accomplished." She motioned around the table. "You have a dentist, a vet, accomplished businesspeople, even a famous actress."

Arnold smiled at her approvingly. "Amber is quite talented herself. Show them one of your sleight-of-hand tricks," he urged.

Amber brushed off the request. "I'm sure your friends don't want to see something silly like that."

"I'd love to see a trick," Phil said.

Amber blushed, but put her camera away in its case. "Pay close attention," she said, then dazzled them with so many innocent-looking gestures and misdirection she had them convinced she could rub a coin into her elbow and make a saltshaker disappear.

"How did you do that?" Cheryl asked.

Amber grinned. "I shifted your attention from what I was really doing. Like when I appeared to accidentally drop the coin before I finished the first trick."

"You did that on purpose?"

Her grin widened. "No move is ever by accident." She squeezed Arnold's hand. "You know that, right?"

"I'm learning."

"Good." She looped her camera gear and purse over her shoulder. "I'll be back. I need to go refresh my lipstick."

A few minutes later, Arnold was telling them a funny story about a bodybuilder who'd fainted at the mere sight of the dental drill when DeeDee stopped by the table. "You wouldn't believe the things I just heard Nina saying to Amber in the restroom," she whispered to Kaylee. "I think she mistook her for Ginger."

Kaylee remembered Amber dancing with Reggie earlier in the evening and wondered how long Nina might have been hovering in the shadows before making her entrance.

"She insisted she knew Amber's type," DeeDee went on in a low voice. "For a minute there, I thought I was going to have to call in Arnold and Reggie to break it up."

"That's probably not the kind of memory Wilma's trying to create with this reunion," Kaylee noted quietly.

DeeDee shook her head. "I can't believe there's as much drama as ever in this class. You'd think they would've mellowed out by now."

"Is the teacher Wilma wanted to honor here?" Kaylee asked, louder.

"Not tonight. But he's going to give us a guided nature hike tomorrow, then stay for the picnic. He's also joining us for the dinner cruise on Sunday, and of course we'll be honoring him in the Hall of Fame Sunday night." DeeDee glanced at her husband, Andy, who was pointing to his watch. "I better get going. Our babysitter couldn't stay late tonight."

"See you tomorrow," said Kaylee.

Cheryl, Phil, and Ewan rose too, and said their good nights.

"Hey, I thought Amber was going to be right back," Arnold said suddenly with an anxious expression.

At the bar, Ginger's bodyguard suddenly seemed very interested in something or someone outside the nearby window. The bodyguard whispered something in Ginger's ear then let himself out the side door.

"I need to make a call," Wilma announced and excused herself from the table.

Reese and Arnold talked about their college days, but as another ten minutes passed with no sign of Amber, Arnold grew increasingly worried.

"I'll go check on her," Kaylee volunteered. "She probably got chatting with someone and lost track of time."

But the women's restroom was empty.

Kaylee scanned the bar area as she headed back to their table, but couldn't spot the redhead anywhere. And Kaylee had clearly missed some action during her brief search of the restroom, because Reggie was now escorting his wife out the front door with a firm hand on her elbow. He offered Kaylee a magnanimous smile as he passed, but it seemed considerably more forced than the charming smiles he'd been passing around before.

Kaylee pushed open the side exit to see if she could spot Amber and was surprised to find it raining. Ginger's bodyguard stood under the protection of the eaves, smoking a cigarette. A couple dashed toward their Honda parked in the back lot. Kaylee slipped back inside and took a longer route through the restaurant so she could scan the other tables on her way back to theirs. Amber had been so talkative with everyone, it wouldn't have surprised Kaylee to find her chatting at another table, oblivious to Arnold's distress.

But there was no sign of her anywhere. She was gone.

3

"What do you mean, she's gone? Where would she go?" Arnold demanded when Kaylee told him his date was missing. He yanked his cell phone from his pocket.

Kaylee met Reese's gaze and knew he thought the situation was as strange as she did. Why would Amber just up and leave without saying anything to anyone?

Remembering the scene with Nina and Ginger, and what DeeDee had said about Nina and Amber's argument, Kaylee asked Reese quietly, "Why did I see Reggie hustling Nina out of here?"

He winced. "Apparently she saw him glance toward Ginger at the bar and went berserk. He subdued her with one doozy of a kiss before hauling her outside. It sure didn't look like the first time he's had to make a quick exit."

Kaylee glanced in Ginger's direction and her gaze momentarily collided with the bodyguard's. His narrowed eyes sent a shiver down her spine as he handed Ginger a bright-pink water bottle.

Arnold's desperate "Amber, where are you?" snapped Kaylee's attention back to their table.

Arnold clutched his cell phone to his ear. "Please. Call me as soon as you get this." He hung up and shifted his gaze to theirs. "She's not answering. What should I do?"

"Maybe she wasn't feeling well and went back to the hotel," Kaylee said.

Arnold flung a handful of bills on the table and got up. "I should check." His phone beeped. He glanced at it and let out a relieved sigh. "It's a text from Amber. She says she doesn't feel well and walked back to the hotel. She didn't want to tell me before she left because she knew I'd insist on going with her and she didn't want to take me away from my friends." He grinned at them. "She's so thoughtful, even when she's not feeling her best."

"Sounds like a great woman you've got there." Reese cuffed Arnold's shoulder encouragingly.

"Yeah. She says I should stay and enjoy myself and she'll see me in the morning." He wavered. "Do you think I should go check on her anyway?"

Wilma returned to the table. "You're not leaving too, are you? It's not even nine yet."

A popular song started and the dance floor began to fill.

"Why don't you take Wilma for a whirl around the dance floor before you leave?" Reese suggested to Arnold, then turned to Kaylee and extended his hand. "Shall we?"

Grinning, Kaylee took his hand. "I'd love to." As Reese led her to the dance floor, she snuck a peek over her shoulder. "Did we convince Arnold?"

"I think so," Reese whispered.

"I'm so glad. Wilma clearly has a huge crush on him. I think she'd love even a few dances."

"Hmm," Reese said. "I wonder if Amber noticed that too."

"You think that's why she left? She wanted to open the field for him?"

Reese shrugged. "Could be. She doesn't seem to be overly attached to Arnold."

"Yeah, I was trying to figure out if it was that, or if she was simply being really conscientious about taking lots of candid shots of the alumni."

"Maybe a little of both. Come on. Let's focus on having fun. Someone needs to show these alumni how it's done."

For the next song or two, they let loose and enjoyed

themselves. Kaylee was a little surprised by Reese's confidence on the dance floor.

"Wow, you're really good at this," she told him.

"You sound surprised." A hint of teasing colored his tone.

Wilma let out a yelp behind Kaylee, and she spun around in time to see the woman take a spectacular spill.

"Oops," Kaylee whispered, "too bad you didn't give Arnold some pointers."

"Watch the floor there," Wilma said to everyone around as Arnold helped her to her feet. "It's wet. Somebody probably spilled a drink or came in from the rain without wiping their feet."

The dance floor emptied and a server hurried over with a rag to wipe it dry.

"I'm afraid I need to call it a night," Kaylee said as she and Reese rejoined Arnold and Wilma at the table. "I have an early flower delivery to make tomorrow morning. I had a great time with you all."

"Good night, Kaylee!"

"Drive safe."

Reese walked her out to her car. "I'm so glad you were here tonight. It helped to know more than just one or two people. And your spectacular dancing was a bonus."

She laughed. "I had a great time too," she told him as he opened her door for her.

"See you soon," he said before closing the door.

She smiled all the way home.

The next morning, Bear pranced excitedly in his seat as they drove past the harbor. She sometimes walked him along the water after buying her morning coffee. "I'm afraid we don't have time today," she said. "I have to make a delivery." She parked at the curb in front of her shop and peered down the street toward the water.

The early morning sun glistened on the rippling ocean waves. "I'll tell you what. We can explore the shoreline near the hotel this morning after I drop off that arrangement. How's that?"

Bear let out a yip of approval.

"Great. Wait here," Kaylee said. "I'll only be a minute." She hurried inside, grabbed the arrangement from the cooler, and raced back out to the car.

Bear had relocated to the driver's seat as if he were ready to chauffeur her around.

"Nice try," she said, shooing him out of her seat. "I'm driving."

When she reached the hotel, she tied Bear to a railing and told him to wait for her while she delivered the flowers to the front desk. Inside, Ginger's bodyguard, who seemed to be returning from a morning run, must have heard her say they were for the actress, because he veered their way. "I'll take those," he said.

"This is Ginger's bodyguard, so I'm comfortable trusting him with them," the hotel receptionist explained, confirming Kaylee's suspicions.

The bodyguard pulled the card from the bouquet and scowled. "Who bought these?"

Kaylee stepped back, stunned by his harsh tone. "I don't know. My employee took the order."

"But you can find his name on an invoice or something."

"If he used a credit card to pay. Why?"

He tipped the floral card for her to read.

"'Wherever you go, I'll be right there with you. M,'" Kaylee read aloud. "You don't know who M is?" On the surface, the note sounded very sweet, certainly nothing that would have raised any red flags when Mary took the order.

A muscle twitched in the man's jaw. "No."

"A stalker?" *Silly question,* she admitted silently when the bodyguard cast an annoyed glare at her. Clearly it was someone trying to creep Ginger out, unless ... "Maybe he thinks she should know what M stands for."

"Yeah, most nutjobs think their targets should know them."

Kaylee winced. "Right, I see what you mean. I'll check that invoice as soon as I get back to the shop."

He pulled a business card from his wallet. "My number is on the card."

She glanced at the card—Dave Griffin. She lifted her gaze to him. Somehow he didn't look like a Dave to her. She averted her gaze and motioned toward the exit, suddenly feeling ridiculously nervous. "I need to go now. My dog's waiting for me outside." As she strode toward the exit, she could hear Dave telling the receptionist to get rid of the flowers.

Bear sprang to his feet the instant Kaylee stepped outside.

"Good boy." She straightened the yellow-and-green striped bow tie she'd put on him this morning in honor of Turtle Cove High's school colors, then snapped on his leash to walk him across the road. Once they reached the rocky shore, she unsnapped the leash and let him run. He sprinted across the rocks, yipping at the seagulls that flew away in a flurry of indignant squawks.

Kaylee closed her eyes and turned her face toward the sun, breathing in the clean sea air. Dave's reaction to the flowers had rattled her. She hated to think that a creep had used her flowers to harass another person—and she also hated to think of them going to waste. Hopefully the receptionist would at least display them at the hotel for some free decor. She took another deep breath and tried to think of something more pleasant. Like how much she'd enjoyed dinner and dancing last night.

Bear's urgent barks snapped her out of her daydreaming. She squinted down the shoreline, trying to make out what was bothering him. A crab had probably snapped at his nose or something. She headed toward him. "What is it, boy?"

After a few steps, she realized that the long red strands twined over the rocks ahead weren't seaweed or grass. Her heart pounded and for a second she froze, not wanting to believe what she was seeing.

It was hair. On a body. One she recognized.

Bear was still barking.

"That's enough, boy." Kaylee raced toward the prone form. "Amber?" Kaylee dropped to her knees at the woman's side. She wore the same clothes she'd had on the night before.

Bear nudged Amber's hand with his nose, but there was no response.

Kaylee's chest squeezed. Tears springing to her eyes, she pressed her fingertips to the woman's neck.

She felt nothing.

"She's gone," Kaylee whispered. She scanned the beach, the water, the road, but there was no sign of any tourists or residents who had potentially seen what had happened. She pulled out her cell phone and dialed 911.

The operator assured her that deputies would be dispatched immediately.

With a whimper, Bear lay down beside Amber and rested his head on his paws.

Kaylee remained at the woman's side too, her mind zigzagging through memories of the night before, trying to figure out how this could have happened. Amber's purse was still slung over her shoulder, so it didn't appear to be a robbery that had taken a fatal turn.

Kaylee studied Amber's hands and arms. There were no

defensive wounds anywhere, at least to her untrained eye. As the sound of sirens approached, Kaylee pushed to her feet. "Ouch!" Bits of broken glass on the rocks had dug into her palm but hadn't broken the skin. She carefully brushed them away, then walked up the slight incline to the road to flag down the emergency responders.

Sheriff Eddie Maddox was in the first cruiser. "You know the victim?" he asked as Kaylee walked him to where Bear had stayed to keep watch over Amber.

"I met her yesterday. Her name is Amber Mason. She came as Arnold Boyer's date for the reunion. We were at the Pacific Street Diner last night. Amber left early."

"How early?"

"Sometime before nine."

"Alone?"

"Yes. She went to the restroom and then just didn't come back. After Arnold called to ask where she was—she didn't answer—she texted to say she'd gone back to her hotel room and that she'd see him in the morning."

"Had they had a disagreement?"

"Not that I saw or heard."

The sheriff nodded, but Kaylee had the sense he wasn't necessarily ready to accept her answer at face value. He squatted next to the body and expressed the same observations she had about Amber's purse and the lack of defensive wounds.

Deputy Alan Brooks arrived with a camera and evidence collection kit.

"I want lots of pictures," the sheriff told him, "before anyone else contaminates the scene. Kaylee, are these the same clothes she wore to the party?"

"Yes." Still disliking his question about whether Amber and Arnold had fought, Kaylee added, "Arnold couldn't have done this. He was with us the whole time."

"Unless they went out for a walk along the shore, after he returned to the hotel."

"In the rain?"

Maddox shrugged. "Maybe he was angry with her for embarrassing him by leaving early. Until Giles can give me a time of death, we can't dismiss the possibility." He was referring to Giles Akin, the local coroner who also ran Akin Funeral Chapel.

Frowning, Kaylee attached the leash to Bear's collar. "That seems like a really extreme reaction, and Arnold seems to be a very stable individual."

The sheriff walked Kaylee back to the road. "Then maybe she simply stumbled on her way to the hotel and suffered a fatal fall. But it'll be some time before I know for sure. I'll want to talk to everyone who interacted with her last night."

Kaylee blew out a breath. "That's practically every person here for the reunion."

DeeDee came out of the hotel and hurried toward Kaylee.

"Let me know if you think of anything else you observed about the victim last night that might be relevant," the sheriff said, then turned back toward the body before DeeDee reached them.

"Hey, what's going on?" DeeDee craned her neck to see past the departing sheriff's back.

"Amber's dead," Kaylee said softly.

DeeDee gasped. "How?"

"Not sure yet."

"That's awful. Poor Arnold. That girl was so sweet. And in the prime of her life too."

Seeing tears in her friend's eyes, Kaylee squeezed her hand. "We're all going to be there for him."

DeeDee clapped a hand over her mouth. "This will put a cloud over the whole reunion. What should we do? Wilma's worked so hard planning it all. You don't think we should cancel, do you?"

"No. Aside from Arnold, the rest of the group only met her last night. I don't think anyone else knew her well enough to grieve her, though the loss of life is always horrible. Besides, the sheriff will want everyone to stick around. He'll need to question everyone who saw her last night. We might as well give them a pleasant reason to stay."

DeeDee's eyes widened. "He thinks she was murdered?"

"He doesn't know what to think yet. He doesn't have enough information to rule out the possibility."

"Do you think Nina went after her after they left?"

Kaylee shook her head. "Reggie was with Nina. He wouldn't have let her do anything stupid. That reminds me. I need to tell the sheriff something." She headed back toward where the police were working. Deputy Nick Durham had joined Deputy Brooks in collecting evidence.

DeeDee chased after Kaylee down the rocky shoreline. "What?"

As they reached him, the sheriff asked, "Did you remember something about last night?"

"Ginger has a stalker on the island—or at least one who knows she is on the island," Kaylee said, answering Sheriff Maddox and DeeDee at the same time. She filled all of them in on what Dave had told her when she delivered the flowers.

DeeDee gasped. "And Amber is a redhead like Ginger. Maybe the stalker mistook her for Ginger the same way Nina did."

Kaylee crinkled her nose, doubting someone who would devote so much effort to tracking the object of his attention would mistake another woman for her. "Her stalker had to know Ginger's bodyguard would never allow her to walk along the shoreline alone."

"Hmm." DeeDee glanced at the body, then frowned. "Wait, where's her camera?"

Kaylee startled. How had she missed that it wasn't there? "That's right. She had it when she left the restaurant last night, or at least when she left our table. Maybe it was a robbery gone wrong after all."

"Or maybe we'll find her camera in her hotel room, because she went out again later in the evening," Sheriff Maddox said. "You did say she called Arnold and said she was back at the hotel, right?"

Kaylee paused as the puzzle pieces that didn't seem to be fitting righted themselves in her mind. "No. She didn't call. She texted. What if it wasn't actually her? And there's no way to know where the phone was when the text was sent. Arnold had just tried to call her. The robber could have listened to the message and figured he'd better send a text to dissuade Arnold from trying to find her. Is her phone in her purse?"

Sheriff Maddox signaled to Deputy Brooks to search the purse, then the pockets of her jacket.

"No phone here," Brooks said.

"What if she left it in her room, along with her camera?" DeeDee suggested. "You know, if she was only coming out for a late-night stroll to clear her head or get some fresh air to make her feel better."

The sheriff stood. "Her hotel key card in the purse?" he asked the deputy.

Brooks shook his head.

The sheriff sighed. "This isn't good." He motioned to Brooks to follow him. "Durham, you stay with the body and wait for Giles. Brooks and I need to get over to the hotel and search the victim's room before the housekeeper starts her rounds."

4

Kaylee and DeeDee trailed Sheriff Maddox and Deputy Brooks toward the hotel, past the cruisers parked along the road. "What were you doing here this morning anyway?" Kaylee asked DeeDee.

"I met an old friend in the hotel restaurant for breakfast. She's here for the reunion." She motioned toward the line of emergency vehicles. "Then I saw all this when I came outside. We should probably tell the sheriff there's a bus scheduled to pick up the alumni for the trip to Cascade Lake in an hour."

"Let's wait to see what he does or doesn't find in Amber's room." Kaylee glanced around the parking lot. "I'm surprised more gawkers haven't assembled. I'd better call Reese to let him know what happened, before he hears it on the news. I'm sure he'll want to be here for Arnold if he can." As she made the call, the sheriff and the deputy disappeared into the hotel.

Kaylee pressed Bear's leash into DeeDee's hand. "Could you hold Bear for me so I can go in? It'd be nice if there's at least one familiar face around when the sheriff breaks the news to Arnold."

"Sure." DeeDee glanced at her watch. "Wilma and Jess should be here soon too."

"You called them?"

"No. Wilma was on her way anyway, and Jess made the desserts for today's picnic, remember? I told Wilma I'd help with it. I have a college student covering the shop for me."

"That reminds me. I need to text Mary and let her know I'll be late getting back to the shop." Kaylee did that as she wandered the hotel hallways looking for the sheriff.

The inn was a well-appointed, three-story building in a style that appealed to clientele who appreciated those little extras but didn't want to pay exorbitantly for them. It was also a good client of The Flower Patch, since they ordered new arrangements of fresh flowers for their lobby twice a week. Not the kind of place where anyone would expect to wake up to news of a dead body.

Unless he or she was responsible for the death. A cold chill ran down Kaylee's spine at the thought.

The elevator dinged and alumni spilled out, chatting amiably.

Kaylee ducked her head and skirted around them to take the stairs.

She let herself into the hallway on the second floor and followed it one way, then the other. No one was in the hallway and only one room door was open. A housekeeping cart sat outside of it and the hum of a vacuum came from its recesses, so the sheriff wasn't in there. Kaylee hurried back to the stairs.

On the third floor, she spotted Brian Cook, the hotel manager, standing outside a room halfway down the hall. Either someone was very unhappy with their room service or it was Amber's room. Kaylee counted on the latter and headed toward him.

"I'm sorry, Miss Bleu." Brian raised a trembling hand to discourage her from coming closer. "I'm afraid we have—"

She met his gaze with empathy. "I'm the one who found the victim."

He winced. "I'm sorry you had to see that."

Kaylee stopped outside the open door and peered in. Her heart lifted at the orderliness of the place. She didn't think it had been ransacked. Maybe Amber had simply forgotten to grab her key card as she left for an evening stroll. Unable to see the sheriff from her vantage point, Kaylee called, "Did you find her camera?"

Sheriff Maddox poked his head out of the bathroom and

scowled at her. "You shouldn't be here."

"I guess that's a no?"

He sighed. "No camera, no phone, no key card, but there's no conclusive sign anyone else has been in here either."

A knock sounded on the room's adjoining door and everyone froze.

"Amber?" Arnold's voice filtered through. "You ready to go for breakfast?"

Kaylee shot Sheriff Maddox an empathetic glance. Telling people a loved one has died had to be the worst part of his job.

Arnold knocked again. "Amber?"

Sheriff Maddox flipped the dead bolt and tugged open the door.

"Oh, you did hear me," Arnold said, his head down as he tapped something on his phone screen. Perhaps he'd been trying to call her. He looked up and stepped back at the sight of the sheriff in Amber's room. "What's going on? Where's Amber?" Arnold noticed Kaylee still standing at the door. "Kaylee? What are you doing here?" His gaze bounced from the neatly made bed to the open curtains on the window to the deputy dusting the bureau for fingerprints. "Where's Amber?" he asked again, his voice cracking.

Kaylee gulped hard and couldn't stop the tears that sprang to her eyes.

The sheriff urged Arnold to step back into his room and sit on the bed. Then he opened the door to the hallway so Kaylee could join them without walking through Amber's room, which they were clearly considering a possible secondary crime scene. The room smelled as if Arnold had been a tad too liberal with his cologne that morning.

"I'm afraid your friend is dead," the sheriff said gently.

"No." Arnold stared at the sheriff. After a long moment, he turned to Kaylee.

Kaylee swiped at her damp eyes.

"No!" Arnold shouted. "No, she can't be. She said she didn't feel well, but she wasn't . . . I should've checked on her. I shouldn't have let you guys talk me into staying longer." He clapped a hand over his mouth, blinking madly as if to stop the tears filling his eyes.

Once he'd calmed down enough to listen, the sheriff explained how, where, and when Amber's body had been found. Then he said, "I'm sorry. I know you're upset, but I have to ask you a few questions. Is that all right?"

Arnold nodded numbly.

"How long have you and Amber been dating?"

Arnold's cheeks colored. "I met her two and a half weeks ago. She joined me in the cafeteria of the building where I lease office space for my dental practice."

"Where is that?" the sheriff interjected.

"Seattle. She'd just gotten a job at a shop down the street." His gaze drifted and his tone grew nostalgic. "We hit it off right from the beginning and shared lunch every day for a week before I summoned enough courage to invite her to dinner." A tiny smile flitted across his lips at the memory. "When I told her about my upcoming reunion here, she said she'd always wanted to visit Orcas Island."

Kaylee's heart flipped over. It was too sad for words.

"So you invited her to join you?" Sheriff Maddox pressed.

"Yes." Arnold ducked his head. "You could have knocked me over with a feather when she agreed."

"Do you know her home address?" The sheriff held his pen poised over his notepad.

Arnold grimaced. "No." He hesitated, as if only at that moment realizing how odd that was. "She always met me wherever we were going."

"How about her employer's name and address?"

Arnold shook his head, then bit his lower lip. "She was always so talkative. Asked me all kinds of questions. I guess I didn't realize how little I'd asked her about herself."

"You don't know where she worked?" the sheriff pressed.

"No."

"But you said it was a shop on the same street as your office. What street is that?"

Arnold provided his office address, and the sheriff copied it down.

"Did she ever mention family?"

"Yes, she has an older brother. I think she said his name was Wyatt."

Brian knocked at Arnold's open door. "Sheriff, one of my housekeepers has found a phone, possibly the victim's. She said she heard ringing coming from the garbage bag on her housekeeping cart and found this." He unwrapped a washcloth that held a smartphone clad with a pink protector.

"I think that's Amber's," Arnold said. "Why would she throw away her phone?"

The sheriff, already wearing latex gloves, took the phone but couldn't get past the password request to unlock it. "Do you know her password?" he asked Arnold.

"No."

In her mind, Kaylee replayed the timeline of last night's events, as the sheriff tried to crack the combination. If Arnold didn't know the password, it was doubtful anyone else did. So maybe Amber had been the one to send Arnold the text after all.

"Arnold, could you dial Amber's number? That way if it rings, we'll at least be able to confirm that this is her phone," Kaylee said.

He complied and the phone rang.

"Perfect." The sheriff handed the phone to Deputy Brooks to

process for prints, then caught the attention of the housekeeper hovering outside the door. "Did you empty the trash from the next room between the time the guest checked in yesterday and this morning?"

"No, sir. Only the receptacle next to the vending machines is emptied on this floor after the rooms are cleaned in the morning."

"And where is your cart stored when it isn't in use?"

"The housekeeping closet."

"Is that door locked?"

She slanted a penitent sideways glance at her boss. "The lock is finicky. Sometimes it doesn't catch."

"Was it locked when you arrived this morning?" the sheriff asked.

"No, sir."

"Thank you. You may go." Sheriff Maddox leaned through the doorway into Amber's room and instructed his deputy to dust the door handle of the housekeeper's closet for prints.

Through the connecting doorway, Kaylee noticed large shoe prints in front of Amber's suitcase set on the case holder. They appeared significantly larger than the impression the deputy's shoes would leave. "Sheriff, did you happen to notice those prints when you arrived?" She pointed toward them.

"Yes, they were here before we arrived. We photographed them and will compare them to those in the vicinity of the victim's body."

"The carpet is still damp there too," Deputy Brooks said. "It was raining last night, so if anyone stood in front of the suitcase to search it, the water in his treads would've seeped into the carpet."

"And those prints are way too large to be from Amber's shoes," Kaylee added.

Arnold's voice rose. "You're saying someone was in her room? Someone could have killed her?"

"Is there any sign of broken bits of glass?" Kaylee asked the deputy as the sheriff attempted to calm Arnold.

"Why?" Sheriff Maddox asked her.

"There was broken glass on the rocks near where Amber was lying. I nearly cut my hand on it."

"There are glass shards on the floor here." Deputy Brooks pulled out a small evidence bag and used tweezers to drop the pieces he'd found into the bag.

"If you keep this up, Kaylee, I'll have to put you on the payroll," Sheriff Maddox said. To Arnold, he said, "Were you in Amber's room?"

He twisted the tissue he was clutching. "I carried her suitcase in when we arrived and put it on the rack."

"What time was that?"

"Shortly after 1 p.m."

The sheriff noted Arnold's answer in his notebook, then glanced at the tissue he'd mutilated. "So before it started raining?"

Arnold stuffed the tissue into his pocket and sucked in a deep breath. "Yes."

"Did you go back in later?"

"No."

"Amber also returned to the hotel room in the middle of the afternoon to wash up and change after she brushed against some hogweed," Kaylee filled in.

"That's right." Arnold flashed Kaylee a grateful face. "She caught up with me at The Flower Patch. Then after dinner, she came back here again on her own. At least . . ." Arnold swiped at the tear that leaked from his eye. "That's what her text said."

"May I inspect your shoes?" the sheriff asked.

"Why?" Arnold sprang to his feet, his cheeks flaming. "I didn't do this. She was my girlfriend!"

"Take it easy," the sheriff said. "You were in her room, so

we need to eliminate your shoe prints from the others we find."

Kaylee glanced at Arnold's shoes and tried to ignore the thought that the sheriff was probably also thinking.

Most victims are killed by people they know.

5

$\mathbf{A}$t the sight of most of the alumni huddled in groups in the hotel's parking lot, watching the activity at the rocky beach across the street, Kaylee drew a deep breath before pushing open the hotel door.

The temperature had already reached the midseventies and the sun was shining brightly.

The chill she felt was a different kind.

DeeDee hurried over to her with Bear in tow and Jessica and Wilma at her sides. "Did they find Amber's camera?"

"No. But her phone turned up in the garbage bag on the housekeeper's cart." Kaylee couldn't hold in a sigh. "It's all pretty suspicious, I'm afraid."

Wilma looked as distraught as if Amber had been her best friend, which surprised Kaylee, given Wilma's fondness for Arnold. "How'd Arnold take the news?"

That makes more sense. Kaylee lifted Bear into her arms and hugged him to her chest. "As well as can be expected. He feels guilty he didn't leave the party to check on her as soon as he got her text."

"That's natural," DeeDee said. "The poor man."

"I talked him into staying at dinner." Wilma stifled a sob with a hand to her mouth and blinked hard. "He's going to hate me."

"No he won't." Kaylee set Bear back on his feet and gave Wilma's shoulder a reassuring squeeze. "We all urged him to stay. We couldn't know. The sheriff isn't even sure if Amber sent the text. For all we know, by the time Arnold got that text from whoever it was, it was already too late to save her."

Jessica shuddered. "I had a bad feeling about today. When I got to the shop this morning, Oliver was all limp." Oliver was her prized lavender geranium. She was convinced he could sense pending doom and warned her by drooping.

The gathered alumni and gawkers speculated on what had happened, and snippets of their theories punctuated the silence that descended on the women.

Wilma stared helplessly from the crime scene to the alumni to the school bus coming down the road. "What should I do?" she asked, her voice tense. "The bus is already here. We're supposed to leave in half an hour for Cascade Lake."

"We need to carry on as planned, of course," DeeDee insisted. "Obviously what happened is sad, but a lot of people came a long way to honor Mr. Fletcher." She brightened a little. "Perhaps we could commemorate Amber for a few minutes at the dinner tonight. Mention how, although she was a virtual stranger to us only twenty-four hours ago, she jumped right in to help us make this a memorable reunion by volunteering to take photographs."

"That would be nice," Jessica concurred.

Deputy Brooks came out of the hotel and hopped up on a nearby bench. "Excuse me, people!" His voice rose above the noise of the chattering crowd, commanding their attention. "We understand you have reunion events planned for the day, but before you head out, we need to get statements from everyone who was at the Pacific Street Diner last night, or anyone who saw Amber at any time after she left."

Groans and complaints rose from the crowd.

"The smallest, seemingly inconsequential detail could be instrumental in helping us piece together what happened," Deputy Brooks went on. "We appreciate your cooperation and patience, as there are a lot of people to work through."

Sheriff Maddox stepped out of the hotel's front door at that point and consulted with Brooks.

"Okay, everyone." Deputy Brooks waited for the murmurs to peter out. "The hotel manager has provided us with tables and chairs in the ballroom. Could you all please come inside now? The bus won't leave without you."

"I guess that answers your question," Kaylee said to Wilma. At the woman's dejected expression, Kaylee added, "Don't worry. Everything will work out."

"I'm sure we'll be at the park in plenty of time to meet up with Mr. Fletcher," DeeDee said, falling into step behind a group of alumni heading into the hotel. "Aren't you guys coming?"

"I wasn't at the restaurant last night," Jessica said.

"The sheriff has already taken my statement," Kaylee added. "And the hotel manager wouldn't want me bringing Bear inside."

"I'm sure he'd make an exception under the circumstances." DeeDee stepped out of the line and lowered her voice. "Don't you think we should hang around and listen in on what people are saying? I mean, if it turns out this was foul play, like the missing camera suggests, we might pick up significant details from people's conversations that the sheriff can't hear."

"Good point," Jessica said. "Kaylee and I can monitor what people are saying when they come out, and you and Wilma pay attention to what they are saying inside."

DeeDee flicked a salute and hurried inside with Wilma.

After the crowd had gone inside, Kaylee filled Jessica in on the events leading up to Amber's departure from the restaurant the previous night.

"Did you notice anyone suspicious hanging about when you went to the restroom to find her?" Jessica asked.

Kaylee closed her eyes and mentally scrutinized the scene as she remembered it. She shook her head. "By the time I came out of the restroom, a lot of people had already left. DeeDee said she'd seen Nina confront Amber a short time before, but Nina's husband was escorting her out by the time I returned to the table."

A pair of ladies Kaylee recognized as alumni emerged from the hotel, chatting loudly. "It was a tragic accident," the one said. "What motive could any of us have had to harm the dear girl? Besides Arnold, none of us knew her before yesterday."

Her companion squinted at the police cruisers along the usually quiet street. "I don't know. Ginger gave her a pretty good tongue-lashing after the pyramid fiasco. Remember? She seemed convinced Amber was paparazzi."

The first woman snorted. "Ginger is paranoid."

"Are they talking about Ginger Andrews?" Jessica whispered to Kaylee.

"Yes."

"Well, her paranoia about paparazzi is probably justified. Remember that paparazzo who was here trailing that celebrity a few months ago and then was back when that funeral director died?"

"Jocko McGee?"

"Yeah, that's the guy. He was at the bakery this morning buying a coffee to go. He probably caught wind Ginger was visiting the island."

"Hmm." *Or he got a tip that a body was about to turn up.* Kaylee shuddered at the thought. They still didn't have firm proof Amber had been murdered.

"Speak of the devil," Jessica said, pointing to a guy mostly concealed in some nearby hedges, his camera aimed their way.

Kaylee pulled Jessica behind one of the hotel's pillars. "I probably shouldn't stick around much longer. Mary is expecting me back at the shop. I was just waiting to speak to Reese before I go. I'm a little worried his friend Arnold might become the sheriff's prime suspect."

"You think he might have done it?" Jessica exclaimed. "Wilma's got a huge crush on the man. He's all she talked about every time she came in to sample my special reunion dessert ideas. If he's a killer, we need to protect her."

"I don't think he is. He seemed genuinely surprised and devastated by the news of her death. And if his shoes had matched the prints in her room, I imagine the sheriff would have already taken him into custody."

"That's a relief, and kind of good news for Wilma."

Kaylee frowned. "Good news?"

"I mean that the guy she likes probably isn't a murderer. And at the risk of sounding horrible, I was thinking that now Arnold's date's out of the picture, Wilma might actually have a chance with him." Jessica gasped. "You don't think Wilma—"

"Not a chance. She was still with us at the restaurant until long after Amber left."

"Yeah, but that doesn't clear her since we don't know when Amber died. Wilma knows where this hotel is, so she might have come here late last night or early this morning and called Amber to see if she wanted to go on a walk or out for breakfast or something. Maybe a thank-you breakfast for stepping up to handle the photography. Plus Wilma might be the only person on the whole island with motive, and a blindingly passionate one at that."

Kaylee couldn't argue with that, not with the image of Amber's cold, lifeless body still so vivid in her mind. After all, people did crazy things for love.

Ginger flounced out of the hotel with Dave on her heels. "The woman was way too nosy. She was snapping photos left, right, and center, not respecting anyone's privacy."

"That's what the reunion coordinator asked her to do," Dave said, the slight edge to his voice suggesting he was losing his patience with his employer.

"All I'm saying is that it's not surprising someone lashed out at her," Ginger said haughtily.

"She could be right, you know." Ewan, the vet who'd been at Kaylee's table last night, had joined them. He squatted to make Bear's acquaintance.

Jessica and Kaylee exchanged glances. It was clear to Kaylee that her friend was every bit as intrigued as she was.

"You know how reunions are," Ewan went on. "Some guy unhappy in his marriage has too much to drink and hits on an old flame. Next thing you know they're lip-locked on the beach, and then Miss Snap-Happy comes along and all he can think about is how much the divorce is going to cost him if his wife gets her hands on the photos."

"It's an interesting theory," Kaylee said noncommittally.

Ewan slapped one of the high school's old baseball caps onto his head. "Would you and your dog like to join me for a walk while we wait for the bus to be released?"

"I'm sorry, but I can't. I need to get back to my shop. Thank you," Kaylee said.

The man nodded and strode off alone.

"Whoa. Miss Snap-Happy?" Jessica repeated once he was out of earshot. "You think he killed her?"

"I'm pretty sure he's single. So what would be his motive?"

"Maybe he tossed out that theory to throw us off. It sure sounded as if he didn't like Amber, based on that nickname."

Kaylee watched his departing back skeptically. "I don't think he really knew her."

"Maybe that's what he wanted you to think. Was he still around after Amber left?"

Kaylee frowned. "No, I think he said his goodbyes around the same time."

"Sounds suspicious to me," Jessica said.

Kaylee turned her attention to Bear, who'd apparently heard Ewan use his favorite word—*walk*—and had started to whine. "Why don't we wait to hear the autopsy results before we start jumping to conclusions?"

"It's kind of sad that no one seems terribly broken up over her death," Jessica said. "I get that no one knew her, but people could at least be a little somber out of respect."

"It is sad. And it'll probably make it extra tough on Arnold." Kaylee glanced at her watch. "I really should get going. It doesn't seem as if Reese is going to—"

Reese and Arnold came around the corner of the building.

"There he is." She was impressed that he'd connected with Arnold when she hadn't even seen him arrive, but more importantly she was grateful that Arnold had a friend to lean on right now. From the expression on Arnold's face, he was grateful for Reese's presence too.

Her relief was short-lived. Jocko McGee strode across the parking lot and straight up to Arnold. "Where did Amber get her drugs?"

Arnold's nostrils flared. "I don't know what you're talking about."

"Move along, Jocko," Reese said. "Turtle Cove isn't interested in your kind of reporting."

Jocko grinned and fingered the strap of the camera hanging around his neck. "Lucky for me the rest of the world is." He made a show of examining their surroundings. "And I seem to be the only reporter around. And my sources tell me Amber OD'd."

The shock on Arnold's face mirrored what Kaylee felt. Never in a million years would she have pegged Amber as an addict.

Reese's quick reflexes stopped Arnold's fist a split second before it would have connected with Jocko's nose.

His smirk broadening, Jocko snapped a quick picture of

Arnold's fury as he backed out of swinging range.

Kaylee was about to intervene when Sheriff Eddie Maddox emerged from the hotel. "What's all this?" he demanded.

"Sheriff, any comments on this tragic death?" Jocko asked, rushing toward him.

Eddie glared at the reporter. "When I'm ready to bring the press in on this, I'll contact them myself. Until then, get out of here before I arrest you for intruding in my investigation and harassing my witnesses."

Jocko tipped the sheriff his trademark grin and strode away, whistling.

"Is it true?" Arnold asked the sheriff, sounding as if his heart was shattering all over again. "He said . . ." Arnold shook his head. "I can't believe it. She wouldn't."

Eddie looked to Kaylee for an explanation.

"Jocko said he got a tip that Amber overdosed," she said quietly.

The sheriff winced. "Apparently we have a leak somewhere."

"It's true?" Jessica asked.

Eddie nodded. "Giles just called to tell me that Amber had high levels of a powerful painkiller in her blood—enough to kill her."

"There's got to be a mistake," Arnold protested. "She never took drugs. I never saw any evidence of it."

"I'm afraid that's not what the tests are telling us," Eddie said softly.

Arnold scraped his hand over his increasingly haggard features. Then, as if searching for an explanation, he turned on the spot, staring first in the direction Amber's body had been found, then at the hotel, then at the sheriff. "Someone with no tolerance to opiates could easily appear to have OD'd merely by coming into contact with the drug—for example, through an improperly discarded pain patch," Arnold said, sounding desperate to convince the sheriff of Amber's virtue.

"How do you know so much about drug overdoses?" Sheriff Maddox asked, sounding as if he thought Arnold was protesting a tad too much.

"I'm a dentist. I need to know about pain med addictions because there have been a lot of cases of people getting addicted after being prescribed them following dental surgery," Arnold explained. "I have to be very vigilant and knowledgeable."

"So you can prescribe these drugs?" the sheriff clarified.

"Yes," Arnold said, then apparently clued in to the intimation behind the question. "But I never prescribed any for Amber. She didn't do drugs!"

"Okay, okay," the sheriff said soothingly.

"She didn't," Arnold repeated to Reese.

Reese assured him they believed him, but Kaylee suspected the sheriff would be checking local pharmacies to find out if a prescription had been recently filled for Dr. Boyer.

Kaylee squeezed Arnold's forearm. "I need to get back to my shop, but you're in good hands with Reese. Take care, and let me know if I can do anything for you."

Wilma and DeeDee, who had come out in time to overhear the exchange between the sheriff and Arnold, tugged Kaylee aside before she reached her car. "You can't leave."

"Why? There's nothing more for me to do here."

DeeDee planted her fists on her hips. "You heard the sheriff. He thinks Arnold killed Amber."

Wilma's pleading gaze clung to Kaylee's. "Please, you have to help him. You know Arnold wouldn't hurt a flea. The sheriff will listen to you."

"The sheriff will follow the evidence."

"But we can help nudge him in a different direction," DeeDee said. "You know he's barking up the wrong tree right now."

Bear gave an indignant sneeze.

"No offense," she said to him. To Kaylee, she said, "We should tell the sheriff about what we know about Nina."

"All we really know about is an argument. That wouldn't prove anything." Kaylee scanned the clutches of people spilling out the hotel doors and heading toward the waiting bus. In the distance, the departing ferry's horn sounded. "Have either of you seen Nina and Reggie this morning?"

"No," Wilma said.

Kaylee raised an eyebrow. "And don't you think that's awfully suspicious?"

6

Kaylee called Mary at The Flower Patch and filled her in on what was happening.

"You should go with the group on their outing," Mary urged. "You're bound to pick up more clues by casually hanging out with the alumni than the sheriff managed to squeeze out of them in his interviews."

"If you're sure you don't mind taking care of the shop alone all day," Kaylee said. "I know how much you love to be in on solving a good mystery too."

Mary chuckled. "I'll be fine. And I'll do an Internet search for Nina and Reggie's pictures and be on the lookout for them here in town."

"Perfect."

Kaylee disconnected the call and tapped her phone against her chin, thinking. Even if it didn't lead anywhere, the sheriff really should know everything she could think of that might relate to the case. "Don't go anywhere yet," she told Reese and Arnold as she passed them on the way to the sheriff, who was going over his notes.

"Remember something?" he asked.

"I don't know if it's true," she told him in a low voice, "but I heard a rumor last night that Nina had checked herself out of the exclusive European spa she'd been recovering at to attend the reunion. When she arrived, she definitely seemed angry her husband had come without her."

The sheriff thumbed through his notes. "What's the last name?"

"I'm actually not sure. Wilma will know. Nina and her husband

Reggie were the prom queen and king of their graduating class."

Wilma must have heard her name, because she and DeeDee joined Kaylee and the sheriff. Wilma confirmed Reggie's and Nina's last name, Blake. Kaylee told the sheriff what had happened when Nina arrived and saw her husband dancing with Ginger. DeeDee described the scene she'd seen between Nina and Amber in the restaurant's ladies' room, shortly before Amber disappeared.

"Do you know where the Blakes are staying?" the sheriff asked Wilma.

"Here at the hotel," Wilma said.

"But no one has seen them since last night," DeeDee interjected and motioned toward the bus. "We've asked everyone boarding for the excursion."

"We'll check into their whereabouts, thank you. No more amateur investigating," the sheriff said sternly. He went back inside the hotel.

"The bus is ready to leave," Jessica said to the group of them still standing on the sidewalk outside the hotel. "Arnold, are you coming?"

"No, I'm going home. I'm not in the mood for any more social activities."

"I can understand why you'd feel that way," Reese said. "But I suspect the sheriff would prefer that you stick around."

"Right. Because he thinks I supplied her with drugs." Arnold kicked at the ground in frustration. "He's crazy."

"All the more reason to stick around and ensure he finds the creep who really killed her, don't you think?" Kaylee said softly.

"Her death's my fault." Arnold's face crumpled, and Kaylee worried that he might break down on the spot. "I never should've invited her. It was nothing more than an ego trip."

"Now who's talking crazy?" Wilma said, her voice kind. "There is no way her death was your fault."

"It was. She wouldn't have been here if it weren't for me." His hands fisted. "All I wanted to do was make myself look good so no one would think I was the same dweeb they knew back in high school."

"No one thought you were a dweeb," Wilma said.

"Yes we did," some guy quipped as he walked by.

Arnold's chest deflated.

Kaylee sent Reese a silent entreaty to do something to convince Arnold to stay.

Reese nudged Arnold's shoulder. "Let's join them. I heard they have a hike planned. It'll help take your mind off of things for a while."

"And we need you," Wilma chimed in again. "You're the mastermind behind re-creating the yearbook photos."

"Amber was the one with the camera," he pointed out dejectedly.

The statement jolted Kaylee's thoughts. The missing camera had to be a clue. If it had been a bad robbery, surely the thief would've taken her purse too. "What other people and places did Amber take pictures of here, besides the alumni?"

Arnold gave a small, wistful smile. "Anything or anyone that caught her eye—scenery, real estate, artsy close-ups."

"It's such a shame we've lost all the reunion photos with her camera," Wilma said. "She took some terrific shots."

"Hopefully the police will find her camera. Maybe we can still get her photos back," DeeDee said encouragingly.

"Kaylee, why don't you take over the official photo-taking duty?" Jessica suggested.

"Yeah," DeeDee said. "You take great candid pictures."

"I don't have my camera with me," Kaylee said, although she immediately warmed to the idea. Viewing Arnold's classmates through the lens of a camera could give her some insight into what Amber might have seen that had made her a target.

"Don't you live around the corner?" Reese asked Wilma. "Do you have a camera Kaylee could use?"

Wilma shook her head. "I use my cell phone."

"You can use Andy's camera," DeeDee said, referring to her husband. "He left it in my car."

Reese nudged Arnold. "We should go along with her. She'll need your advice on what pictures to re-create."

"Oh yes," Wilma agreed. "Of our senior year hike at the park."

"We've reserved the log pavilion in the day use area next to Cascade Lake," Jessica said. "You know how quickly the parking lot there fills up on a gorgeous summer day like this. So are any of you riding the bus? Wilma and I have the food in coolers in my trunk, so we're driving ourselves."

"I can take everyone else," Kaylee volunteered.

"Sounds good to me." Reese opened the back door of her Ford Escape and motioned Arnold in before he could protest.

It occurred to Kaylee that they might have picked up more clues by listening in on conversations during the bus ride, but there'd be plenty of opportunities to do that the rest of the day.

Kaylee was ushering Bear into the back seat with the men when the sheriff marched out of the hotel. "What happened?" Kaylee asked, seeing his grim face.

"Reggie and Nina aren't here."

"They checked out?"

"No. And their luggage is still in their room."

"They could have gone out somewhere for breakfast," Kaylee suggested.

"But the bus was supposed to leave an hour ago," DeeDee said. "They should have been back by now."

"I've issued a BOLO for them," the sheriff said. "Unfortunately, it's too easy to sneak off the island in a private boat."

"Were there two suitcases in the room?" Kaylee asked. "Because Nina came in separately."

"Yes, two large cases and a small one."

That didn't sound as if one spouse was shipping out without the other. "We'll let you know if they turn up at Cascade Lake," Kaylee said. "We're heading there now."

Jessica pulled up alongside them and Wilma hopped out of the passenger seat as the sheriff gave Kaylee a curious frown. "Why are you going? You didn't attend Turtle Cove High."

"The Petal Pushers volunteered to help out," Wilma interjected.

The sheriff bristled, as if he could divine why Kaylee was really going. "Yeah, I bet you did," he grumbled so only she could hear.

Kaylee smiled innocently at him and climbed into her car.

Wilma caught DeeDee's arm before she had a chance to climb into the passenger's seat and whispered something in her ear.

The next instant, DeeDee stuck her head in the car and said, "I just remembered I still have to grab the camera from my car. Why don't you take Wilma with you and I'll hitch a ride with Jess?"

Wilma bustled into the passenger seat, full of grins, and pulled on her seat belt. "I thought we might brainstorm some of the photos we can take."

"That's a good idea," Reese said from the back seat as Kaylee put the car in drive. She didn't miss his relief at having reinforcements to help cheer Arnold.

Wilma chattered on and on about funny incidents that had happened during class trips to the state park, not seeming to notice that Arnold scarcely offered more than an occasional nod or grunt.

Moran State Park, with its scenic lakes, nearly forty miles of trails, and fabulous views—especially from the top of Mount Constitution—made it one of the most popular park destinations in the San Juan Islands. As Kaylee passed under the welcome arch, Bear barked excitedly in the back seat and Kaylee felt herself start to relax for the first time since finding Amber's body.

By the time they reached the day use parking area, it was almost full. Youngsters dashed toward the beach carrying towels and sand pails, while others eagerly lifted kayaks or paddleboards from car roofs, and still others gathered up their rods and tackle.

"Do they still stock the lake?" Arnold asked somewhat absently. But it was encouraging to see him taking an interest, nonetheless.

"Oh yeah," Reese said. "I caught a gorgeous pair of kokanee salmon here earlier in the summer. You still like to fish?"

Arnold shrugged. "It's been years."

"Maybe we should plan a weekend camping trip here this fall," Reese suggested.

"Yeah, maybe," Arnold said, his voice flat.

"There's our bus." Wilma pointed to the far end of the parking lot.

By the looks of it, the alumni had already exited the bus and were milling about.

Wilma opened her window and called, "Don't go too far. We'll meet at the trailhead for the Cascade Lake Loop in ten minutes."

Conversations drifted in through the open window as Kaylee hunted for a place to park.

"Can you believe the guy's luck?" a short, stocky bald man asked of a bespectacled beanpole.

"Now? Yeah," the beanpole replied. "But not when he showed up with that knockout on his arm yesterday. I mean, I knew dentists made gobs of money, but no one likes them."

"Yeah, I heard they have one of the highest suicide rates."

Kaylee thumbed the window button to shut out the conversation and sincerely hoped Arnold had missed it. Glancing in the rearview mirror, she caught Reese's eye, and he gave her a subtle nod of thanks.

She sincerely hoped this group wouldn't spend the entire

afternoon gossiping in their same old high school cliques. That would only make Arnold feel worse.

"I think that's them," Wilma said, twisting in her seat as Kaylee apparently passed by whoever it was as she circled the lot.

"Them, who?"

Wilma shot a glance to Arnold in the back seat, then whispered, "Nina and Reggie."

Reese, smart guy that he was, distracted Arnold with another fish story as Kaylee started another circuit. *Surely there's one space left. There has to be.*

"You're right. It is them," Kaylee said softly. "Once I park, can you occupy Arnold for a few minutes? I'd like to chat with them before anyone else gets a chance."

"Good plan," Wilma said, sounding a little too eager.

Finally, an empty spot appeared and Kaylee pulled in. As they all exited the vehicle, she told Reese where she was headed. He handed her Bear's leash, then scooted around the nearby cars to where Nina and Reggie watched their former classmates from a picnic table.

"Hey," Kaylee said. "You two missed all the action back at the hotel this morning."

"We drove across the island to watch the sunrise," Reggie explained. "Then went out for breakfast."

"What action?" Nina asked.

Suddenly realizing that she was acting like a gossip, exactly the opposite of how she'd hoped the alumni would behave, Kaylee sucked in a deep breath. She had to tell them now. Besides which, she wanted to gauge their reaction to the news. "It's very sad, actually. Arnold's girlfriend was found dead on the beach across the street from the hotel this morning."

Nina gasped.

Reggie wrapped a protective arm around her shoulders.

"What happened?"

"The sheriff isn't sure yet," Kaylee said, deciding to omit the drug finding.

"How's Arnold doing?" Reggie asked. "He must be heartbroken."

"Yes he is." Kaylee glanced in the direction she'd left him. "The sheriff is questioning everyone who was at the restaurant last night to try and piece together what happened after she left."

"I'm sorry, but I wouldn't be of any help," Nina said. "I didn't even meet the woman."

"Actually, you did. She's the redhead you confronted in the restroom."

"Darling!" Shock tinged Reggie's voice.

The color in Nina's cheeks suddenly rivaled that of Amber's hair.

"You've got to learn to control that jealous temper," Reggie scolded, then planted a kiss on her forehead. "You know you're the only woman for me."

At that moment Ginger and her bodyguard roared into the parking lot in a cherry-red Maserati. Climbing out, Ginger fluttered her fingers at Reggie. Thankfully, she was out of Nina's line of sight, although Ginger's smirk said she wouldn't have cared if Nina had noticed.

To his credit, Reggie ignored the flirtation. "So we should pay the sheriff a visit when we get back to town?" he asked Kaylee.

"Yes," Kaylee said. "I'm sure he'd appreciate it. Well, I'd better get back and see if Wilma needs a hand with anything. She wants to start the hike in ten minutes." Kaylee withdrew, relieved that she didn't have to tell them outright that the sheriff was trying to find them. She stopped beside her vehicle, out of view of most everyone around, and phoned Sheriff Maddox.

"Thanks for letting me know," he said, after she'd finished relaying her conversation with the couple. "I'll cancel the BOLO and wait to hear from them if you're confident they aren't a flight risk."

Kaylee's heart dropped a beat. Was she confident?

Nina had seemed genuinely surprised by the news, and her husband made no attempt to downplay his wife's jealous temper—only her justification for it. But maybe they were simply good actors. Kaylee didn't really know them. How could she know if they were flight risks?

"Kaylee?"

"Um, yeah, Sheriff, that should be fine," Kaylee blurted. As she hung up, it dawned on her that if the Blakes were guilty and escaped, it would be entirely her fault.

7

After promising the sheriff she'd let him know if Nina and Reggie suddenly left or if anything else suspicious came up, Kaylee rejoined the others. Jessica and DeeDee volunteered to handle setting up all the food and supplies in the kitchen shelter so Wilma could join her class for the hike.

Wilma glanced at her watch. "Mr. Fletcher should be here by now. He was always a stickler for punctuality."

Arnold glanced around at his former classmates, who all seemed content to meander about the picnic area and chat. Ginger and Dave had wandered to the beach, and another group studied the trail maps. "I don't think anyone's too worried."

An ancient green Pontiac rolled into the parking lot and someone called out, "Fletcher's here!"

The conversation level rose several decibels as a group of the guys rushed toward him. "Can you believe he's still driving that old thing?" one said.

Another laughed. "It's a collector's item now." The guys gathered around their former teacher, shaking hands as they reintroduced themselves.

Mr. Fletcher beamed at the enthusiastic welcome.

Wilma made her way through the crush of gathering alumni and thanked him for joining them. "We can get started on the hike whenever you're ready."

He gave her a curt nod, then clapped his hands. "All right, class, follow me!" He led them to the Cascade Lake Loop trailhead.

Kaylee gave Bear's leash a little tug. "Want to go for a walk?"

He yipped and pranced in a circle.

DeeDee handed her Andy's DSLR camera. "Keep your ears open. You might pick up some clues. Jessica and I will keep an eye out here and make sure no one's up to anything suspicious." She winked and turned back to the shelter.

"Here, let me take Bear." Reese relieved Kaylee of the dog's leash. "You'll have your hands full snapping photos."

The trail, like all the trails in the park, was beautiful, but they needed to watch their step for roots. At one point, Bear suddenly jumped as if he'd mistaken one of the twisting roots for a snake.

Reese chuckled. "I guess I won't have to worry about him running off after a deer."

"I doubt we'll see any today," Arnold said. "The group's making too much noise."

"What's that hammering?" Wilma asked.

Mr. Fletcher stopped and turned toward the group. "That's a pileated woodpecker." He scanned the massive Douglas firs surrounding them, then suddenly pointed to one. "There it is. See the redhead?"

Kaylee snapped half a dozen photos of it from various angles.

"It's huge," one of the women gasped.

"The males grow as large as 19 inches," Mr. Fletcher said. "But this one's a female."

"How can you tell?" Reggie asked.

"The males have a red cheek stripe. This one's is black."

It let out a loud laughing sound that made Bear jump several feet in the air, then start barking at it. The bird spread its wings and flew off.

Oohs and ahs echoed through the group.

As the hike continued, Ewan stepped up on Kaylee's other side and whispered, "Let's hope we don't see any vultures."

Kaylee opted to ignore the unwelcome reminder of that morning's grisly find and focused instead on Mr. Fletcher's discussion of the local flora and fauna.

He stopped at a small clearing and told a story about copycat plants—how weeds closely resembling desired plants inevitably grow up alongside them, counting on their look-alike quality to spare them from the hoe. "They steal space, nutrients, and sunlight from the plants we want to cultivate. These invasive species operate the same way and have become a threat to our native plants here," he said. He pointed to an example in front of him but seemed to be struggling with the name.

Kaylee spoke up. "That's *Geranium lucidum*, or shiny geranium. It has only spread to Washington in the last decade or so. It's hard to eradicate because it can survive in several different kinds of habitats. It likes to grow with its cousin *Geranium robertianum*, also known as herb Robert, next to the ones Mr. Fletcher pointed out."

"Wow," Ewan said. "I had no idea florists knew so much about the scientific side of flowers."

"I'm sure many do, but I was also a plant taxonomy professor and forensic botanist before coming to Turtle Cove to take over my grandmother's flower shop."

"Like CSI stuff? Did you help the police solve crimes?" a woman asked.

Kaylee chuckled. "Yes, as a matter of fact, I did consult on a number of investigations."

"Did the sheriff ask you to consult on the investigation in Amber's death?" the woman asked.

Kaylee glanced at Arnold and winced at having inadvertently steered the conversation in such an uncomfortable direction. "No. My particular expertise isn't likely to offer much insight in her case."

"What kind of things might a forensic botanist find at a scene that could help the police solve a crime?" Ginger asked.

Her bodyguard hissed something to her out of the side of his mouth.

"I was only curious," she huffed.

"Curiosity is good," Mr. Fletcher said. "Can you give us an example?"

"If pollen, spores, seeds, or plant remnants not indigenous to the scene are present, they could indicate where the perpetrator had been prior to his or her arrival. Or on the flip side, pollen or spore evidence unique to the scene might later be found on a suspect's clothes when he or she claims he was never there."

A woman nodded. "I saw that on a television program."

Kaylee smiled, since TV shows rarely showed the details accurately. "I also worked a case where soil samples left behind by a shoe tread pinpointed a unique location where the shoe's owner had been, since the soil shared the same composition profile. Tire treads can often give police good information in the same way."

"That is so cool," Ginger said. "It's a wonder they ever managed to solve any crimes before they could test for all this stuff."

"Actually, a botanist testified in a big case way back in 1935. His name was Arthur Koehler, and he specialized in forestry products. He was able to match the wood in a homemade ladder used in the kidnapping of Charles Lindbergh's son with a partial floorboard in the kidnapper's attic. The direction of the tree's growth, the pattern from the mill where it was planed, the surfaces of the wood, and the grain all matched."

"That's amazing," a woman murmured.

"We'd better carry on," Wilma spoke up, "so we make it back in time for our picnic."

Mr. Fletcher resumed his lecture on habitats as they resumed hiking. When he reached a large tree, he stopped. "Does anyone recognize this tree?"

"It's a *Pinus contorta*," Kaylee responded when no one else did. "Lodgepole pine."

"Yes," Mr. Fletcher said, "but this time I was referring to the class's relationship to this particular tree and all of its neighbors." He waved to the rows of similar trees around it.

Cheryl gasped. "Are these the saplings we planted?"

Mr. Fletcher smiled. "They are indeed. This section of the park is your own contribution to its reforestation."

"Wow, I can't believe how big they've grown," Cheryl said.

"Nice to see something that put on more flesh than me in the past couple of decades," a man quipped. The others laughed.

"We should reenact the picture we took for the yearbook!" Wilma exclaimed. "Everyone stand by a tree."

Most of the alumni gamely ambled over and stood proudly beside a tree—perhaps the one they'd planted all those years ago. Reese nudged Arnold forward into the picture, then helped Kaylee set up the shot.

After she'd taken a few photos, Mr. Fletcher drew his class's attention to the foliage surrounding the base of the trees. "See how different plants and grasses are growing here than in the surrounding forest. Who can tell me why?"

Kaylee grinned. It was fun to see how taking the man out of the classroom didn't take the teacher out of the man. She was surprised by her own urge to share her knowledge about such disturbed habitats as she would have with her university classes not so long ago. She missed seeing the light in students' eyes, sparked by new knowledge.

Wilma's hand shot up. "Because the new trees created a new habitat favoring different plant species."

Mr. Fletcher smiled broadly and nodded. "It's so nice to see that my students remember some of what I taught."

The class laughed.

"This kind of difference in plant species between nearby plots of earth can also be a clue that helps investigators identify clandestine graves," Kaylee interjected and scanned the faces of the group. She added a silent apology when she caught Arnold's eye, but she had to see if this kind of talk made anyone nervous. "Whenever soil is disturbed, certain plants quickly take root in the fresh dirt, followed by others, so that the composition and distribution of plants in a disturbed area is never exactly the same as the surrounding earth."

"The presence of a buried body could also change the chemical composition of the soil," Mr. Fletcher remarked, "which might further inhibit or promote certain plant growth."

Arnold shivered, misery plain on his face, and Kaylee felt even guiltier. Couldn't she have come up with a different way to make Amber's killer reveal him- or herself? Preferably out of Arnold's hearing?

"I wouldn't want to commit a crime with you two around," Nina said.

Arnold whispered something to Reese and turned back toward the picnic area.

"I better go with him," Reese said softly to Kaylee. "I can hang on to Bear though."

Wilma's gaze followed them longingly, but she stoically continued on with the rest of the group.

"Hey," someone blurted, backing away from a Queen Anne's lace plant and pointing. "Is that one of those hogweeds you were talking about yesterday?"

"No, that's *Daucus carota* or wild carrot," Kaylee said. "Hogweed is much taller and the flower heads are the size of a dinner plate."

Ginger hugged her arms close to her body. "I need to head back to the lake."

"You're in no danger from these plants," Kaylee reiterated.

"That might be, but I can't risk exposing myself to anything that'll give me a rash."

Phil chuckled. "Yeah, or you might spend several episodes of that soap of yours in a hospital bed, wondering if they're going to write you out."

Ginger's gaze flared. "It's no laughing matter." She flounced back in the direction they'd come, even though they were already almost halfway around the loop.

Dave hurried after her.

"Who is that guy?" Nina asked. "Half the time he follows her around like a lost puppy. The rest of the time he follows her like a pit bull."

"He's her bodyguard," Reggie said.

"Oh brother." Nina rolled her eyes. "Talk about an ego trip. He's for our benefit, to show off how big and important she's become?"

"Actually," Kaylee countered, "she's had issues with a stalker harassing her."

"That's got to be scary," Ewan said. "Do you think he managed to track her to the island?"

Kaylee shrugged noncommittally. "Anything's possible." She stopped herself before she divulged that she believed the stalker had placed yesterday's flower order. She wasn't sure Dave planned to tell Ginger about the flowers, or whether he meant to keep her blissfully in the dark as long as he could. Given the gossipy tendencies the alumni seemed to have, it was best not to give them information she wasn't sure should be passed along.

"If he did track Ginger here," Ewan mused, "he could have attacked Amber. She and Ginger are both redheads. What if he mistook her for Ginger?"

Kaylee's heart pounded at the reminder of her own initial theory. Had she been too quick to discount it?

Feverish whispering arose among the group as they debated its merits.

"I think I'll head back now too," Phil said to his wife. Kaylee noticed that his limp had gotten more pronounced.

"You want me to come with you?" Cheryl asked.

"No, you enjoy the time with your classmates. I'll wait for you back at the beach."

After Phil left, Kaylee saw Cheryl draw alongside Reggie and engage him in conversation. Not that that in itself was surprising—everyone seemed to be switching positions periodically to catch up with different classmates as they walked. What was surprising was that Nina didn't seem bothered by her husband talking to Cheryl. After last night's displays, Kaylee would have thought Nina would be glued to her husband's side whenever another woman was within twenty feet of him.

At the opposite side of the lake the trail came to a Y. Mr. Fletcher pointed up the side trail. "That would take us to the lagoon."

"I don't think we have time for a side trip today," Wilma said and several alumni were visibly relieved. With the warming temperatures, not to mention the hills, more than a few appeared to be starting to fade.

It was almost comical, since Mr. Fletcher, who was both fighting an illness and had more than forty years on all of them, was probably in better shape than half the class.

He didn't say much from that point, besides pointing out the odd bird or interesting plant, allowing them to finish the second half of the loop in about half the time they'd taken for the first one.

When they got back, the alumni devoured the fabulous lunch Jessica and DeeDee had ready for them, then changed into swimwear to enjoy the beach of Cascade Lake.

"We had a sandcastle-building contest here when we came our senior year," Wilma told Kaylee. "So if I can convince some people to try their hand at it again, please take lots of pictures."

"Will do," Kaylee promised.

Wilma persuaded a large group of the alumni to participate, then coaxed Arnold, who had returned, into helping her build one.

Kaylee snapped several shots, then made her way over to Reese, who'd opted to watch from a shady spot at the edge of the beach with Bear at his side.

"Bear seemed a little too eager to help dig up the sandcastles people are building," Reese said with a smile.

Chuckling, Kaylee squatted beside them and rubbed Bear's ears. "You wouldn't do that, would you?"

"Would and did. Those two had a good start before Bear decided to 'help,' but now . . ." Reese waved toward a couple whose sandcastle was considerably smaller than the competition's.

Kaylee laughed. Her eyes fell on the dentist. "How's Arnold doing?"

"He's an emotional roller coaster."

"That's understandable. Hopefully by the time we get back to Turtle Cove, the sheriff will have a solid lead."

"That would be good."

Kaylee stood. "I should get back to taking pictures." She focused the camera in on each one in turn. As the viewfinder skittered over Cheryl sunbathing on the beach, Kaylee cringed. "Whoa. I'm thinking someone didn't put on her sunscreen. I'd better say something to her before she gets any worse."

As Kaylee got closer, she realized the blisters on Cheryl's arm were no ordinary sunburn. "Cheryl? I'm afraid you might have come into contact with the sap of a *Heracleum mantegazzianum*."

"What?"

"A giant hogweed," Kaylee translated. "See this rash on your arms? The sap makes skin dangerously sensitive to sunlight. If you don't get out of the sun now, these blisters could leave nasty scars.

You should get back to the hotel right away. Change your clothes and wash, then see a doctor for something to help with that."

"But we came on the bus," Phil said.

"Then I'll drive you," Kaylee said. "We need to take care of this as soon as possible. It can get much worse far too quickly."

Phil hurriedly gathered up their belongings and then coaxed Cheryl toward the parking lot.

As they passed the kitchen shelter, Jessica intercepted them. She worriedly looked from Cheryl's worried face to Kaylee. "What's wrong?"

"I need to get Cheryl back to town so she can see a doctor. I'm pretty sure she's come into contact with hogweed," Kaylee said.

"After you told Ginger there wasn't any hogweed here," Phil griped.

"There isn't any that I'm aware of," Kaylee admitted. "All the more reason for her to have the blisters checked by a doctor, in case I'm wrong and it's from something else."

"I can take them into town," Jessica said. "All my coolers are loaded and I was about to head out anyway." Jessica nodded to the camera hanging around Kaylee's neck. "Besides, I think they'll want you to take more pictures of the sandcastles."

Kaylee thanked Jessica and headed back to the beach, only to run into Ginger and Dave heading toward the parking lot. Ginger's face was ashen, and she started at Kaylee's unexpected appearance.

"What happened?" Kaylee asked.

The woman's gaze darted every which way. "I need to go."

Kaylee caught Dave's gaze. "Is the stalker here?"

Ginger froze. "You know about him?"

"She's the florist he ordered the flowers from," her bodyguard said.

Kaylee clapped a hand to her forehead. "I'm so sorry. With finding Amber's body and everything I completely forgot to ask my assistant to check out his payment info for a name." She pulled out her phone. "I'll do it right now." She texted the request to Mary. "How do you know he's here?" Kaylee asked, even though they hadn't actually said he was.

"He left a note in my beach bag," Ginger said.

Kaylee shivered.

"And there's no way he managed to slip it into her bag between the hotel room and the car," Dave said. "He probably passed by while it was sitting next to the picnic table or her beach chair and dropped it in."

Kaylee's phone chimed a text alert. Kaylee glanced at the screen. "I'm afraid he paid cash for the flower order and never left a name."

Dave nodded. "I'm not surprised."

A second text immediately followed. "Mary says she remembers he was lanky and blond, and nicely dressed in chinos and a golf shirt," Kaylee added.

Dave squinted toward the beach. "A few guys here fit that description. Give me a call with the license plate if one of these guys follows us."

Kaylee nodded as she quickly typed another text to Mary: *Was the guy an alum?*

Mary's response was immediate. *He was not one who came through the flower shop during yesterday's town crawl, so as far as I know, no.*

Kaylee scanned the beach, but couldn't spot any blond, lanky guys who weren't also part of the reunion. "What did the note say?" Kaylee asked.

Ginger shuddered and turned away.

Dave recited the note quietly. "It said, 'See what walking a quiet beach alone at night gets a girl? You should think twice next time you claim you want to be left alone.'"

8

As Ginger and Dave drove off, Kaylee turned from the parking lot and started snapping pictures of the entire area. Whoever had put the note in Ginger's bag was doubtless still here and maybe she or Dave would recognize his face. He'd clearly been stalking her for a while. They had to have seen him a time or two, even if they didn't realize it. And if it turned out this guy had killed Amber . . .

Mr. Fletcher strolled up to Kaylee, a paperback novel tucked under his arm. "Why's everyone leaving so soon?"

"Not everyone. Ginger doesn't like to be out in public for too long. You know how it can be for celebrities."

He snorted. "All that tabloid nonsense is ridiculous. The girl always did everything she could to garner people's attention. Now that she has it, she doesn't want it." He shifted his chin to the dust trail still lingering behind the disappearing car. "Was that Cheryl who left in the other car?"

"Yes. I'm afraid she came into contact with *Heracleum mantegazzianum* and contracted a nasty rash."

He tipped back his brimmed khaki hat and stared down the road, shaking his head. "Cheryl was always my brightest student. I can't believe she'd be so inattentive to the flora around her as to expose herself to hogweed."

Kaylee shrugged. "Everyone is pretty excited about catching up with old friends. They probably aren't paying much attention to where they're walking."

"But she was the only student who could tell a *Conium maculatum* from a *Pastinaca sativa*. Probably saved another student's life because of it too. Since the silly boy thought tasting the plant would be a good way to aid identification."

"Yikes." Kaylee grimaced. People died every year by accidentally ingesting hemlock. Both plants had fernlike leaves, so it wasn't surprising someone would mistake hemlock for wild parsnip. They were all in the carrot family, as was hogweed. "I'm sure she'll pay more attention from here on out."

Toward late afternoon, the bus driver announced it was time to return to town, and the remaining alumni gathered up their beach towels and bags.

True to his apparent golden touch, Reggie won the sandcastle-building contest. As they paused to admire Reggie's masterpiece, Bear bounded over the moat and tore into the highest tower with joyful abandon.

For an instant, everyone seemed to hold their breath, unsure how the prom king would react. Fortunately, Reggie burst into laughter. The rest of his former classmates immediately joined in. Kaylee lifted the camera and shot a video of Bear's demolition project and his laughing audience.

"It's going to take me a week to get all the sand out of his fur," she groused to Reese as everyone headed for the bus.

He grinned. "I thought it was good of him to break some of the tension of the day."

"Then you can give him his bath."

Arnold, Wilma, and DeeDee opted to take the bus back to town, so Kaylee and Reese stopped in at the sheriff's office on the drive back to find out how the investigation was going and what he thought about Ginger's stalker.

Dave and Ginger had turned in the note, and the sheriff was treating the whole thing with surprising skepticism.

"You don't think her stalker had anything to do with Amber's death then?" Kaylee asked.

"I'm not dismissing the possibility, but my gut tells me her stalker merely capitalized on the incident to frighten Ginger."

"Did you dust the note for fingerprints?" Kaylee pressed.

"I do know how to do my job." Eddie's tone held a hint of amusement, reassuring her he didn't mind the questions. "We only found Ginger's and her bodyguard's prints on it. And the paper was from one of the hotel's notepads."

"The stalker is staying at the same hotel?" Kaylee's voice squeaked, and if the realization scared her, what must it be doing to Ginger?

"Or he wants her to think so," the sheriff said. "He seems to enjoy tormenting her."

Which makes him even creepier in my book. Kaylee thought about the lack of prints on the note and squinted at the sun. "It's a hot day. You'd think we would've noticed someone wearing gloves on the beach."

"Her stalker might have held the note inside a tissue or his beach towel or a book—any number of things."

Kaylee frowned. "Pretty much everyone there carried stuff like that."

Reese betrayed his frustration when they returned to the car. "This investigation is going nowhere fast."

"We only found her this morning. We need to be patient. Something will give the culprit away."

"I hope so. For Arnold's sake." Reese glanced at his watch. "I'll have to grab my truck as soon as we get back to Turtle Cove. I have a small job I need to finish for a client."

"No problem. I need to relieve poor Mary at the shop."

The drive back to town was a quiet one, both of them lost in thoughts and worries. Kaylee was grateful to escape into the haven of The Flower Patch. Hopefully work would take her mind off things.

But business was slow, so they closed the shop a few minutes early, leaving Bear to nap on his bed, and joined the rest of the Petals for coffee in Jessica's shop. The girls were eager to be caught up on anything Kaylee knew about the case, so she filled them in on the note Ginger had received and the sheriff's reaction to it—quietly, so as not to disturb Wilma, who was working on a laptop at the next table.

"Did you see the latest tabloid?" Mary picked up a paper left behind on one of the tables. The headline read: *Ginger Andrews Shops for New Home on Old Stomping Ground.*

"This kind of speculation just because someone pays a place a visit must drive celebrities crazy," Kaylee said.

"There might be some truth to it," DeeDee said. "I saw her looking at the boards in a real estate agent's window down the street."

"Yeah, that's probably all the reporter saw too." Kaylee skimmed the article over Mary's shoulder. "That doesn't necessarily mean anything. Half the people who walk by those boards stop to peruse them."

Jessica put a finger to her lips, then pointed to a customer in a booth by the window—Jocko McGee, the reporter who had written the story, according to the byline.

"That's interesting," Mary said, perusing the rest of the article. "It says Ginger has been straining to avoid the public eye in recent months. I wonder what that's about."

"She was in a nasty car accident six months ago—missed weeks on her soap," DeeDee said.

"Ginger got pretty irate with Amber about photographing her," Jessica recalled. "Maybe angry enough to spike her drink in retaliation?"

"That's possible," DeeDee said. "Amber was floating from table to table introducing herself and taking pictures. And maybe

Ginger's bodyguard fetched both Amber and Ginger a drink from the bar. If Amber felt light-headed, it would explain why she suddenly decided to return to her hotel room."

Kaylee swirled the coffee in her cup and stared at it contemplatively. "If Ginger was in a car accident and using painkillers, I would think her bodyguard would be making sure she wasn't overdoing them."

"I don't know," Jessica said. "If he wanted to keep his job, I think he'd do whatever she told him to. Maybe even spike a snap-happy person's drink."

And then plant a note in Ginger's bag to divert suspicion from them? Was that the real reason only their prints were on the note? "Was Amber behaving as if she didn't feel well when you saw her in the restroom?" Kaylee asked DeeDee.

DeeDee frowned. "No, not that I noticed."

"Then we really have no reason to suspect anyone of spiking her drink."

"Except that those pain meds had to get into her system somehow," Mary said.

The conversation flagged as they all waited to be struck by sudden insight into what had happened. Kaylee glanced over at Wilma. "What are you working on?"

Wilma blew a wayward hair from her face. "Frantically trying to sift through all the photos alumni are e-mailing me before tonight's mini-golf tournament. I've already managed to send a current photo of each alumni to the printer to pull together the commemorative collage I want everyone to sign for Mr. Fletcher, but if we're going to have a digital montage of all the other photos by tomorrow night, I need to get a head start."

Kaylee moved behind Wilma and studied each picture as it loaded, searching for potential clues to who might be connected to Amber's death. There had to be a couple hundred or more.

After Wilma had scrolled through the last of them, Kaylee said, "It's too bad none were taken outside the restaurant last night. Maybe we'd have been able to spot Ginger's stalker lurking around."

"Yeah, too bad." Wilma glanced at her watch and closed her laptop. "I've got to run. Were you guys going to come to the mini-golf tournament?"

"I can if you still need a photographer," Kaylee said.

"It's fine. I coaxed Arnold into doing it. Reese thought it'd help keep his mind off the investigation."

"Good idea," Kaylee said. Reese had constructed several of the newly revamped holes at Albatross Mini Golf, which had probably helped him convince Arnold to go along. "I'll pass if you don't need me. I still have a couple more special decorations I want to make for tomorrow's dinner."

"That's awesome. Thank you." Wilma tucked her computer into her shoulder bag and hurried out of the shop.

The moment the bell above the door jangled upon her exit, Jocko McGee set down his coffee mug with a clank. "I was there last night."

"Taking pictures?" Kaylee clarified.

"What do you think?" He patted the camera slung over his shoulder. "Never go anywhere without this baby. She's my stock-in-trade."

"Could we see the pictures?" Kaylee asked.

He leaned forward and planted his elbows on the table. A tiny smirk played on his lips. "For a price."

Kaylee offered him her sweetest smile, pulling out her cell phone. "Or I can let the sheriff know you probably have evidence in the case, and you can negotiate with him." She made a show of scrolling through her contacts and struck a contemplative tone. "Although since he and the judge are fishing buddies, I'm pretty sure he could secure a signed search warrant in the time it takes him to drive here."

"Touché. I like your spunk, Kaylee." Jocko chuckled and leaned back in his chair, stretching out his long legs. "You can put away the phone. I'll show you what I've got."

Kaylee reined in her grin and did as he asked. Sure, he was probably as keen to see what she might deem significant in the photos, but this way she got to see his pictures for herself. If Jocko got the potential lead on a juicy story out of it, so be it.

"Wait a second." Jessica disappeared into a back room and soon returned with the laptop from her office. "You can view them on this. They'll be easier to see than on the tiny screen of his camera."

Jocko removed the SD card from his camera and inserted it into the slot on the side of Jessica's computer. Thumbprints for more than 2,000 photos filled the screen.

"You've taken all of these since arriving in Turtle Cove?" Mary asked, squinting at the screen from behind Jocko's chair.

"Gotta love digital. It's a whole lot cheaper than film, so I can snap photos of anything I think might be important. And every one is time stamped."

Recognizing pictures of the beach at Cascade Lake in the thumbnails at the bottom of the screen, Kaylee had another idea. "Could I see the pictures you took this afternoon first?" She hadn't noticed him at the park, but if he had wanted to catch Ginger in an uncensored moment, that was no doubt how he preferred to operate.

Jocko obligingly scrolled to his most recent photos and, with a knowing smile, paused on a photo of an ashen-faced Ginger handing Dave a note. "Is this what you're interested in?"

Kaylee's pulse quickened. "Yes, can you scroll back?"

Jocko did as she asked. "Who wrote the note?"

"We don't know. I was hoping you'd caught him on film slipping it into her bag."

"Ah, one sec." Jocko highlighted Ginger's beach bag in the image and with a couple of clicks on the keyboard instantly compiled all the images that had captured the bag. Unfortunately none showed anyone but Ginger or Dave anywhere near it.

Kaylee sighed. "Can you bring up your pictures from last night?"

Jocko brought back the screen of thumbnail images and scrolled to the photos taken after seven the previous night.

A hundred photos in, there were several pics of Ginger's bodyguard having a smoke outside the restaurant.

"Hey," DeeDee said as Jocko clicked through them. "Go back."

He did and DeeDee pointed to a woman standing in the shadow of the building. "Is that Wilma?"

Jocko zoomed in on her image. "Looks like she's on the phone."

"Yeah, I remember she went out to make a call after Amber left the table," Kaylee said.

Jocko clicked through two more pictures and stopped at the third. "And what do we have here?"

Amber was talking to Ginger's bodyguard. Judging by their body language, it wasn't a friendly conversation.

DeeDee tapped the edge of the screen. "Zoom over here. Is Wilma still standing in the shadows?"

Jocko zoomed in on the shadowy wall of the restaurant. It came in highly pixelated, but with a little contrast enhancement, he pulled out the image of Wilma still standing there, clearly frowning in Amber's direction.

"Did Wilma say she saw Amber outside the restaurant?" Jessica asked.

Kaylee slanted a glance at Jocko, who seemed equally eager to hear the answer. "Not to me," Kaylee said softly.

Jocko scrolled through the remaining photos taken outside the restaurant. They showed various people coming and going, including the departure of Nina and Reggie, as well as Phil and Cheryl. But none of the photos had captured any potential stalker lurking in the shadows, watching Ginger or anyone else through the windows—unless you counted the man behind the camera lens.

"Satisfied?" Jocko asked. He popped the SD card from the computer without waiting for a response and slid it back into his camera, then stood. "If you'll excuse me, I have a mini-golf tournament to catch. If I catch a few shots of Ginger with a golf club, I can do a piece about how movie stars are just like us. Readers eat that stuff up." He hustled out the door.

For a good minute or more, Kaylee, Jessica, Mary, and DeeDee stared at each other in stunned silence. DeeDee was the first to break the silence. "I know how this appears, but I know Wilma. She wouldn't hurt a soul."

"I don't know," Kaylee mused. "She's harbored a serious crush on Arnold for decades. It had to be irking her to see Amber with him and pretty much ignoring him. Maybe her righteous indignation at how Amber was treating him kicked in. And she went too far in carrying it out."

"How would she have done it?" Mary asked. "Does Wilma have access to such potent pain meds?"

DeeDee frowned. "A bookshelf in the library broke last year, smacking her with an avalanche of books that left her with a pretty serious concussion and whiplash that still flares up from time to time."

"So she could conceivably carry pain meds with her at all times, just in case," Jessica said.

"I guess." DeeDee shook her head. "We're talking about Wilma here. I don't see it. I'm dizzy simply thinking about all the work she's put into making this weekend special for her classmates and Mr. Fletcher. How could someone with that much dedication to others be a killer?"

Kaylee pulled a pen from her purse and commandeered a napkin from the dispenser in the middle of the table. "Let's go through who left the restaurant when."

DeeDee recounted the names of a few alumni Jocko had captured leaving the restaurant, prior to or soon after Amber. Among them were Phil and Cheryl.

"They didn't seem to have any animosity toward Amber," Kaylee said. "Can you think of any possible motives?"

"No," Jessica said, "Nina and Ginger seem to be the only ones with obvious motive. Nina clearly thought Amber was getting too cozy with her husband, and Ginger was furious over all Amber's picture snapping."

"Yeah," DeeDee said, "and Nina is probably spiteful enough to try to spike someone's drink."

"Do you think it's possible she did it without Reggie noticing?" Jessica asked.

"Some people are very good at hiding things," Mary said. "I can't tell you how many times that came in when I was a 911 dispatcher."

"And like I said before," DeeDee added, "Ginger's bodyguard had opportunity to spike her drink."

"Hang on," Kaylee said. "We're forgetting a couple of things here. Amber was still carrying her camera in those pics Jocko shot outside the restaurant, and I think we can assume she still had her phone too. So whoever spiked her drink must have also followed her, waiting for the drug to take effect, in order to take the camera and phone and then text Arnold." Kaylee sighed. "And I hate to say it, but Wilma didn't return to the restaurant until after Arnold got the text, so she's not in the clear."

"What about Ginger's bodyguard?" DeeDee asked. "When did he come back inside?"

Kaylee closed her eyes and raked through her memories of that night. He'd met her gaze as he came back inside and gave Ginger her personal water bottle. Where had he gotten it? Perhaps he'd gone to their car before coming back inside. Jocko's pictures hadn't shown that. "I remember Arnold was preparing to leave when he got the text alert," Kaylee said. "And the bodyguard was already back inside."

Kaylee wrote *camera* on the napkin followed by three question marks. "We've forgotten something that's got to be connected to the killer's motive. Why'd her killer take the camera?"

"Maybe her death and the theft aren't connected," Mary said. "Maybe someone like Ginger or Nina or Wilma drugged her out of spite and, not feeling well, she left and texted Arnold, but on the way back to the hotel, she collapsed. Then someone else came along after she died, saw a valuable camera, and helped himself rather than call the police."

Kaylee frowned. Her friend might be right, but her gut told her that whatever was on the camera was significant.

9

Without more clues, chances were slim they'd be able to prove anyone killed Amber. And the last thing Kaylee wanted to do was upset DeeDee more with suspicions about Wilma. Kaylee returned to her shop to finish assembling the special arrangement Wilma planned to present to Mr. Fletcher at Sunday's award ceremony.

As Kaylee poked stems into the florist foam, her thoughts flittered back to last night's dance. What if the wet spot Wilma had slipped on hadn't been on the floor at all, but on her shoes? She'd gone outside to make a call, and it had been raining. But according to Jocko's photos, she'd stood under the overhang, where her shoes were unlikely to have gotten wet. But they would have gotten wet if she'd trailed Amber.

Kaylee closed her eyes and tried to recall who else had been on the dance floor. The guests at their table and nearby tables had had to walk across the dance floor or skirt around it to leave the restaurant. And Wilma was the only one who'd later returned to the table. But had Ginger's bodyguard walked across the dance floor? His shoes could have gotten wet from fetching Ginger's bottle from her car.

Kaylee poked a flower into the foam a little too forcefully and snapped the stem. She yanked it back out and tossed the two halves into the trash can, along with her speculations. After all, neither would have had time to also go to the hotel and search Amber's room. And Wilma's feet weren't nearly as large as the shoe prints in front of Amber's suitcase. Of course, whoever had snuck into the room could have done it much later when the risk of being spotted going in or out was negligible.

"That's it!"

Bear startled and cocked his head.

"We need to see the inn's security tapes." Kaylee quickly finished the arrangement, then locked up the shop and bustled Bear out to her car.

"Where are you racing off to?" Jessica asked, coming out of her shop.

"Turtle Cove Inn. I want to see if their security cameras picked up anyone sneaking in a back door in the middle of the night using Amber's key card."

"You mean like someone who isn't staying there for the weekend?" Jessica asked. "Don't you think the sheriff would've already scrutinized the inn's security tapes? In fact, given all the locks are electronic, they should be able to search the records for which key card was used where and when."

"Talk about Big Brother creepiness. But yeah, maybe the system does create a record, which means the records could tell if someone used Amber's key card to access her room after her death too."

"But didn't the sheriff already get those records?"

"Maybe," Kaylee said. "No harm in asking."

"True. I'd join you, but Luke made dinner reservations for us, so I need to get home."

"No problem. I'll let you know if I learn anything." Kaylee took the long way around to the inn so she could drive past the mini-golf course. It wasn't as crowded with players as she'd expected. Many of the alumni had apparently opted for a quieter evening.

By the time Kaylee reached the inn, Brian, the manager, was walking out to his car. Kaylee parked in the first available spot and flagged him down. As he veered her way, she quickly hooked the leash on Bear's collar and let him out of the car.

"What can I do for you?" Brian asked.

"I was wondering if the sheriff has seen the surveillance tapes of the inn's entrances to see if someone might have come in who shouldn't have."

Brian grinned, his eyes twinkling. "I'd heard you were a bit of a sleuth."

Kaylee shrugged. "A little, I guess."

Brian nodded. "The sheriff did take copies of the surveillance tapes. I also skimmed through them and didn't see anyone entering or leaving who wasn't a registered guest." He inhaled deeply. "Trust me. I'd hoped to, because it'd be a whole lot easier to put a palatable spin on 'Guest's Stolen Key Used to Gain Access to Hotel Room' than 'Hotel Guest Kills Fellow Guest.'"

"I can see how one of those headlines might be better than the other for you. Do you know if your key card system tracks which key opened which door and when?"

Brian bopped his forehead with the butt of his hand. "I can't believe I forgot to check. The sheriff asked me the same thing." He spun toward the inn's entrance. "I told him I didn't know because I'm still pretty new and I've never had to use a feature like that, but I'd check it out and get back to him. Let's go see if we can find out."

Kaylee paused outside the door. "Is it all right if my dog comes in?"

"Sure," Brian said, holding the lobby door for them. "He won't bother anyone." He squatted and straightened Bear's green-and-yellow striped tie. "Besides, you could be the school mascot in that cool tie, so none of the alumni would dare complain."

Bear licked Brian's chin and tugged Kaylee through the door.

Chuckling, Brian slipped past them in the lobby and led the way to his office. "There must be a way to view the key cards or door locks' time stamps. I've just never had to do it before and I'm not very techy. The last hotel I ran still used metal keys."

Phil and Cheryl walked past as Kaylee and Bear reached the manager's office. "Phil, look at the cute little dog with his bow tie," Cheryl cooed. She glanced from Kaylee to Brian, who'd already moved behind his desk and wiggled his computer mouse to wake up the computer. "Skipping the mini-golf tournament?"

Kaylee nodded. "Since I'm not part of the class, I didn't feel it was my place. And Wilma didn't need help with anything. How about you? How are you feeling?"

Cheryl gingerly plucked at the long blousy sleeves covering her arms. "Uncomfortable, but the doctor says I got out of the sun quick enough that with proper treatment, the burns shouldn't leave any scars."

"Thanks to you," Phil added. "I'm sorry I blamed you earlier. It wasn't your fault."

Kaylee smiled. "I understand. I'm sorry it spoiled your day."

"The doctor said as long as I stay out of the sun, I should be fine. We'll be able to join in most of tomorrow's activities." Cheryl sounded excited about the prospect.

"Glad to hear it. Wilma has some fun surprises planned."

"Well, we won't keep you. See you later!" The couple waved and left, and Kaylee slipped into the office.

Brian already sat behind his computer, tapping keys. "I'm afraid this is going to be more complicated than I expected."

"You found the logs?" Kaylee rounded his desk to see the computer.

"I did, but they're all coded." He pointed to the screen. "See, for example, card number 8-301-2 accessed the rear door at 2:05 a.m. But I don't know whose key card that is."

"I don't know what the eight is for, but my guess would be the middle number is the room number the card accesses and maybe the last number is the copy number, since some guests ask for more than one key to their room if they are sharing it."

Brian clicked the mouse around on other links in the program. "You're probably right. There's got to be a way for me to see the list of key codes by guest or room." He opened a pull-down menu and clicked on *Rooms*.

A long list of numbers filled the screen. "Ah," Brian said, understanding dawning in his voice. "The first number must be the month the key code was issued. See" —he pointed to a column of numbers—"these are the rooms for the alumni, and they all start with an eight for August. Only the key card for rooms 103 and 207 start with a seven. Both those rooms have guests who have been here since July. And like you said, the middle number corresponds to their rooms."

"Go back to the first screen you had," Kaylee said, excitement rising in her chest. "Let's see if Amber's key card, which would be 8-307-1, opened her room between eight o'clock last night and eight o'clock this morning."

"Yes, once at 8:51 p.m."

"That's around the time Arnold received a text from Amber's phone. Wilma came in as he was about to leave and said it wasn't even nine yet." Kaylee scrunched her forehead and mulled that over for a moment. *There's no way Wilma snuck into Amber's room at 8:51 and got back to the restaurant before nine.* "I suppose Amber could have let herself in and sent the text. Has the sheriff told you whether Giles has an estimated time of death?"

"No he hasn't."

"If she died later, it's possible she went back out again after returning to her room, but that doesn't explain the shoe prints in front of her suitcase in her room. You're sure the room wasn't accessed any time after that?"

"Not until I used my master key to open it this morning."

"You probably should call the sheriff. I'm sure he'll want a copy of these logs."

Brian clicked the print icon, and the printer on a stand next to the desk whirred to life.

"I can drop these off at the sheriff's office on my way home," Kaylee offered, hoping Eddie might share the autopsy report in return.

"Thanks. I'm ready to be home myself." Brian handed her the logs, and she and Bear headed outside.

Bear scampered along beside her back to the car. He dropped his nose to the ground as they neared the vehicle, then sniffed the front tire on the driver's side and yipped. "Good boy," Kaylee said. "You found the right vehicle." She let him in and waved to Brian as he emerged from the inn.

"We have one more stop to make and then we'll head home," Kaylee told Bear as they drove. Admiring the view of West Sound, she tapped the brake as she rounded a curve in the road.

A sudden *bang* made her jump. The steering wheel jerked left, and the car swerved across the middle line right into the path of an RV.

Kaylee wrenched the steering wheel back toward her lane.

The thrust of the air mass in the RV's wake thumped the side of Kaylee's vehicle as it sped past.

"Talk about close!" She pulled to the side of the road and shifted the car into park. Twisting toward the back seat, she asked, "You all right, boy?"

He wagged his tail, confirming they'd both escaped the crazy swerve unscathed.

"Stay here." She lowered all the windows a few inches to keep him comfortable. "I'm going to see if I can figure out what happened." The instant she stepped out of the vehicle, she spotted the problem. Her front tire had blown. She knelt down to examine it and found a long nail pushed through the rubber.

Bear scratched at the side window.

"Take it easy. I need to change the tire." She pulled the spare and the jack from the back and set to work. The lug nuts were stiff and even with her extra-long lug wrench, it took all of her strength to get them loose. Glancing at her watch, she grimaced. At this rate, she might have to drop by Sheriff Maddox's house if she wanted to speak to him.

She worked steadily and was almost finished when a cruiser came toward her and, turning on its emergency lights, parked behind her car. Sheriff Maddox stepped out of the vehicle. "What's wrong?"

"I blew a tire, but I should be good now." She tightened the last lug nut and straightened. "Thanks for stopping though. I was on my way to see you with some data the manager of Turtle Cove Inn and I were able to pull off his system."

Eddie glared at her. "So you went back to the hotel after I told you to stop snooping. Do you even hear me when I talk?"

Kaylee grinned at him. "Hearing and listening are two different things, you know."

He sighed. "What kind of data?"

"The times Amber's room was accessed with her key card."

"I guess I should thank you for saving me some time, but I'm worried it'll encourage you. Not that you need it. Follow me to the station." He rolled her blown tire to the back of her vehicle and tossed it in.

Kaylee laid the jack and lug wrench beside it and noticed a second person riding in the passenger seat of the cruiser. She didn't recognize him but waved anyway in a silent thank-you for his patience.

He responded with a curt nod and then averted his gaze.

"That's Amber's brother," the sheriff said. "I just picked him up from the ferry."

"Oh, then this probably isn't a good time for me to come in."

"Nonsense. If you have information that might shed light

on what happened to his sister, I'm sure he'll be eager to hear it too." Sheriff Maddox climbed back into his cruiser and pulled out ahead of her.

By the time Kaylee parked outside the sheriff's department and walked Bear inside, there was no sign of the sheriff or Amber's brother. She stopped at Aida Friedman's desk and smiled at the minty smell that always surrounded it, thanks to her love of wintergreen-flavored Tic Tacs. This week's bouquet of carnations from The Flower Patch adorned her desk, bright and cheerful in the otherwise spartan room.

"Hi, Aida. Sheriff Maddox is expecting me."

"Hey, Kaylee. Yes, he said to send you straight back to his office." Aida rubbed Bear's ears, even though she was more of a cat person, with three of her own.

"Thanks." Kaylee and Bear headed down the hallway.

Sheriff Maddox poked his head out of his office door and waved her over. "Kaylee, this is Wyatt Mason, Amber's older brother." He motioned toward the dark-haired young man she'd see in the cruiser, who rose and extended his hand.

Kaylee's heart cracked at the sorrow in his red-rimmed eyes. "I'm so sorry for your loss."

He sighed and sank back into his chair. "I warned her this would happen one day."

Kaylee sat in the chair beside his with Bear at her feet as the sheriff rounded his desk to claim his own seat. "So she did have a drug problem?" Kaylee asked softly.

"What? No!" Wyatt's eyes flared and his gaze shot to the sheriff. "Amber never touched drugs. Wouldn't even take ibuprofen for a headache."

"Significant levels of pain medication were found in her system," the sheriff said somberly. "Giles believes they contributed to her death."

"I thought you said she die▨▨▨ blow to the head."

"Yes, a brain hemorrhage app▨▨ to be the primary cause of death, but Giles says the levels o▨▨ meds in her system would have caused her to grow dizzy an▨ ▨riented and could explain her fall on the rocky beach."

Wyatt shook his head vehemently. "I don't ▨▨▨ it. If Amber had pain meds in her system, someone spiked her ▨▨ or forced them on her somehow." He turned to Kaylee. "The ▨▨ iff said you had information that could shed light on the inves▨▨ ▨n?"

"I hope so." Kaylee opened the folder with the pri▨▨ and passed it across the desk to the sheriff." Amber's room ▨ accessed by her room key at 8:51 p.m. That's very close to the time Arnold received a text from her phone."

"So you think she returned to her hotel room and then went out again?" Wyatt asked.

Kaylee didn't know what to think. Who had sent the text— Amber or the person who'd taken her phone? And if Amber had used her key card to return to the room just before nine o'clock, who had left the shoe prints in front of her suitcase and how had he gotten in there?

Her heart stumbled. There was one other way into Amber's room that didn't require the key card—through the door to th▨ adjoining room. Arnold's room.

"She probably went back to her room to change into someth▨ more suitable," Wyatt murmured in a tone that sugge▨▨ ▨ was theorizing.

"More suitable?" the sheriff asked.

"To follow up on whatever she'd seen." W▨ ▨▨ ▨ his head. "I told her it was only a matter of tim▨ ▨he ticked off the wrong person."

"▨▨▨ ▨▨▨▨ asked in unison.

▨▨▨ ▨▨ ▨▨ ▨▨ and back again, surprise

widening his eyes. "You don't know what Amber did for a living?"

The sheriff leaned forward over his desk. "We were told she worked at an office in Seattle."

"No, she worked out of her apartment." Wyatt shrugged. "But that office could be the location of her latest client."

"What kind of client?" the sheriff demanded, clearly losing his patience.

Wyatt met his gaze. "My sister was a PI, a private investigator."

10

Kaylee gaped at Amber's brother. "Amber came to Orcas Island as part of an investigation?"

"I can't say for sure." Wyatt stared down at his hands twisting in his lap. "Last I'd heard she was hired by an insurance company to trail a guy who'd filed a disability claim."

"And you think she followed him here?" Sheriff Maddox asked.

"It would explain why she asked so many questions," Kaylee mused aloud.

"And maybe why her camera was stolen," the sheriff added.

Kaylee returned her attention to Wyatt. "But your sister came here with a date."

Wyatt's eyebrows shot up in surprise, then he shook his head. "It had to be someone she dragged along as a cover to explain her trip. If she was serious enough about a guy to go on a romantic getaway, she would have told me."

Kaylee frowned. Had Amber used Arnold? Maybe Amber wasn't as forthcoming about her romantic interests as Wyatt would like to believe. Kaylee didn't tell her sister about her dates—not that she'd had many since she'd moved back to Orcas Island.

"Who's this 'boyfriend'?" Wyatt wanted to know.

"They met a couple of weeks ago at a coffee shop and started getting together for lunches, then for the odd dinner date. When she heard he had a school reunion here, she said she'd always wanted to visit, so he invited her."

Wyatt nodded. "Is the guy on disability?"

"No. H̶e̶'̶s̶ ̶a̶ ̶d̶e̶ntist with his own practice."

coffee shop, and lunch with the dentist proved to be a convenient cover," Wyatt said with a certainty that was presumably born out of past experience. "She probably already knew the dentist had a connection to where her subject was planning a trip. She has an uncanny ability to find out anything about anybody. You said it was a school reunion? Maybe both men went to the same school."

Kaylee exchanged a glance with the sheriff. Was one of Arnold's fellow alumni the subject of Amber's investigation? And her killer?

"I think we better invite Dr. Boyer back for another chat," the sheriff said. He pressed the intercom button and asked Aida to call Arnold Boyer and ask him to come in.

"He's playing miniature golf with everyone else," Kaylee said. "I can text him."

Wyatt stiffened. "Sounds like he's real torn up over my sister's death," he said, his tone scathing.

"He is," Kaylee assured him. "He was talking about going home because he didn't feel like having a good time anymore. But he needed to stick around in case investigators had more questions, so a friend of his from college who lives here now has been trying to keep him occupied and involved. It won't help anyone, especially him, if he holes up in his room and lets grief consume him. We were concerned Dr. Boyer would drive himself to despair blaming himself for inviting Amber here in the first place."

Twenty minutes passed before Arnold showed up with Reese, a period of time filled with more questions and awkward silences. The sheriff asked Kaylee and Wyatt to wait in the waiting area while he spoke with Arnold privately. As Kaylee passed Arnold in the hallway outside the sheriff's interior office, Reese's questioning gaze captured hers from where he sat in the lobby.

Bear scampered ahead of her and planted his paws on Reese's

knees with a happy yip. Reese grinned and greeted the dog. "I'm happy to see you too."

Kaylee introduced Reese to Wyatt and they all took seats in the waiting area.

After expressing his condolences, Reese said, "Have they figured out what happened? Is that why Eddie wanted to talk to Arnold?"

Kaylee let out a long sigh. "Not exactly. Wyatt believes Amber's only—or at least predominant—interest in Arnold was as a cover for her trip here." Now that Kaylee thought about it, Amber hadn't acted at all romantically inclined toward Arnold. She'd spent the majority of her time flitting from one photo op to another or chatting with other people. Kaylee had figured Amber was simply dedicated to the job she'd agreed to do, but now it seemed that Amber had actually been investigating.

Reese stared at her, stunned. "But Arnold adored her. He told me he thought she was the one. He knew it had only been a few weeks, but he thought they'd clicked."

Kaylee's heart ached for the poor guy. The news wouldn't do anything to help his already fragile state. She and Wyatt filled Reese in on Amber's occupation and current case, at least as much of it as Wyatt could guess.

"We could be wrong," Kaylee said. "Unless Amber kept a diary or something, there's probably no way to be sure of her true feelings about Arnold."

"No!" Arnold's angry shout echoed down the hall.

"Doesn't sound as if he's taking the news well," Wyatt said softly. "I can't say that I blame him, especially if he was as serious about her as you say."

Arnold stomped into the waiting room. "Let's go," he barked at Reese.

Kaylee bustled outside after them with Bear in tow.

"The sheriff says Amber used me. Played me!" Arnold ranted to Reese.

"He doesn't know that for a fact," Kaylee said from behind them.

Arnold spun around and glared at her. "What do you know about it?"

"Hey, hey," Reese said, wrapping an arm around his friend. "She's trying to help."

"It's what Amber's brother thinks, but it doesn't mean it's true," Kaylee said.

Arnold shrugged out of Reese's hold. "Well, the sheriff believes it. And he thinks I figured it out." Arnold's hands fisted at his sides and his face turned three shades of red. "He all but accused me of killing Amber in a fit of rage over it!"

Whoa. Kaylee's heart rate kicked up a few notches. She exchanged a glance with Reese, who seemed equally unnerved by this side of Arnold. If he had discovered last night that Amber had come with him to investigate a case, would he have reacted as furiously?

Kaylee wouldn't have believed it possible until now. But was this how he might have reacted? After all, his emotions were already heightened with his girlfriend's death and his being suspect in her murder. What had pushed him over the edge? The sheriff thinking he was capable of murder? Finding out Amber might have been using him? Or was he angriest with himself for being duped?

A cruiser pulled into the parking lot, prompting Reese to nudge Arnold toward his truck. "Let's go back to my place and talk about this in private."

Arnold's body seemed to deflate and he dejectedly shuffled toward Reese's truck.

Walking beside him, Reese glanced over his shoulder at Kaylee and mouthed, "I'll call you later."

Kaylee waited until they'd pulled out of the parking lot, then marched back into the sheriff's office. "Was that really necessary?" she demanded.

"I needed to know what he was capable of, given ample motive," Eddie said unapologetically.

"He didn't know. There was no change in his behavior last night to give the slightest indication that his feelings toward Amber had chilled," Kaylee snapped. "You basically performed an experiment on him. 'Hey, if I poke him like this, he reacts like that.' He's not a lab rat, Eddie. He's dealing with a lot of really difficult emotions right now. I probably would have reacted the same way if I found out the person I thought I was in love with was not only dead, but apparently had only been using me."

"The facts could have come to light after he left the restaurant."

"He was with us for more than an hour after Amber left. Do you have a time of death for her yet?"

"Probably between eight thirty and ten thirty, which is a wide enough window for Arnold to have left the restaurant and lured Amber out for a moonlight stroll on the beach."

"In the rain? Besides, the key card records don't show her leaving her room again," Kaylee countered.

"They wouldn't, because you don't use the key card to leave, only to enter."

She should have thought of that. "So we need to check the records for Arnold's room. See when he returned from dinner."

"Maybe he simply called from outside and invited her to join him, only returning to his room after their walk. I haven't checked yet," the sheriff said.

Kaylee was starting to get a strong taste of the frustration Arnold probably felt with his questions. "But if the records show he entered his room within ten minutes of leaving the restaurant, that would clear him, right?"

"Perhaps. There's a chance he happened upon her on his walk

home. Maybe saw her investigating and overreacted when she came clean about her true motives for joining him on the trip."

"But that doesn't explain the pain medication in her system. Using a drug to incapacitate her sounds premeditated, not like a crime of passion."

The sheriff rubbed his chin and nodded. "With every theory we come up with, there's always one puzzle piece that doesn't seem to fit."

"Which simply means we haven't happened upon the right theory yet," Kaylee reasoned.

Eddie rose, signaling the end of the conversation. "I appreciate you bringing the key card data to me. And calm down. I'm not ready to arrest Dr. Boyer. I intend to speak to Amber's clients and find out whether she was investigating someone who might have been willing to silence her to keep her from talking."

Kaylee picked up a fish sandwich and fries to go from O'Brien's on the way home, and then, even though it was the end of August, started a fire in her fireplace to help chase away the chill that had set into her bones from the moment she'd learned Amber was a PI. If even she felt a little exploited or taken advantage of by Amber's alleged deception when she'd barely known the woman, was it any wonder Arnold, who'd clearly adored Amber, should feel so angry?

But she couldn't believe he'd learned the truth before tonight and killed her. Although believing that the subject of Amber's investigation might have done so did nothing to settle Kaylee's nerves either.

The wind rattled the eaves.

Kaylee brought the phone next to her grandmother's favorite chair by the fire and snuggled under a blanket to await Reese's call.

A knock at the door yanked Kaylee out of a snooze. "Coming," she called. She glanced out the window on the way to the door. Darkness had fallen. Who would be dropping by this late?

A familiar voice sounded outside. "Kaylee? It's Reese."

Kaylee invited him in and made them each a cup of tea. "Sorry, I thought you were going to call. Otherwise, I would have had this done already."

"I know, but I decided I'd rather talk face to face. I should have checked with you first, though. I wasn't thinking."

"It's all right. How's Arnold doing?" she asked as they settled in front of the fire, Bear on the floor between them.

"Not good. He's petrified the sheriff is going to arrest him. He really wants to get off the island as fast as he can, but he knows it'll only make him look guiltier. And he's devastated that what he thought he had with Amber was all an act."

"So you don't think what he's doing now could be an act?" Kaylee didn't believe it herself, but she had to ask, even after so staunchly defending him to the sheriff. "You know, to cover up a rash act?"

"No. Definitely not. I spent the entire day with him. Nothing he said or did makes me suspect he knew Amber wasn't the wonderful woman he thought she was, up until the moment he walked into the sheriff's office and Eddie dropped the bomb."

"I didn't think so either." She sipped her tea.

"What was Eddie thinking with that little stunt anyway?"

"I think he was trying to see what kind of reaction the news would get."

"Arnold's a person, not some kind of lab experiment," Reese said indignantly.

Kaylee nodded. "I told him something similar."

Reese gave a bark of laughter. "Somehow I have no trouble believing that." Then he sobered. "I'm still worried, though. If a guy like Jocko McGee gets his paws on that story, it could ruin Arnold's reputation, even if Jocko doesn't have any facts to back it up. Arnold's dental practice might never recover."

"I never thought of that. Hopefully, Eddie will be able to get Amber's client records and figure out who she followed here. Fast."

"Yeah, but who's to say that's who killed her? Maybe someone else she's been investigating followed *her* here."

Kaylee groaned at the sheer number of possibilities. "Let's hope she didn't have many other ongoing investigations. The sheriff will need an alibi from everyone she's currently investigating."

"Or maybe has ever investigated, if it was a revenge killing," Reese pointed out.

"I'm hoping the fact that her camera was taken means the killer didn't want her sharing the pictures with anyone, which would suggest it's someone from a current case. She already would have exposed a previous case, so someone she had already investigated wouldn't need to silence her. They wouldn't have anything to hide anymore."

"I was thinking about those pictures. If the killer is still on the island, I wonder if we could draw him out by making it seem like the sheriff's department found her backup of the images."

"That's an idea. Do you think Eddie would go for it?"

"It probably depends on how much he actually knows and how desperate he is." Reese set his empty mug on the side table. "Of course, now that Arnold knows his relationship with Amber was a hoax, Eddie's got to figure rumors will spread through the alumni like wildfire."

A sudden thought jerked Kaylee to attention, and she almost spilled hot tea into her lap. "Reese, if the killer was worried about whatever Amber caught a picture of on her camera, what about all the snapshots the alumni have taken?"

Reese gritted his teeth. "Good point. If the killer knows we're e-mailing them all to Wilma, she could be in danger. As could anyone who's taken photos this weekend."

Kaylee gnawed her bottom lip.

"What are you thinking?"

Kaylee filled Reese in on the pictures Jocko had showed her and the Petals—pictures that showed Wilma frowning at Amber after she left the restaurant. "You know she has a major crush on Arnold. And it's not that I could imagine her hurting anyone, but if she was worried someone had snapped something incriminating, asking everyone to e-mail her copies would've been an ingenious way to screen them."

"Except collecting everyone's photos was Amber's idea, not Wilma's."

"You're right. I forgot." Kaylee frowned, not quite ready to scratch Wilma's name from the suspect list.

"What kind of photo do you think would incriminate Wilma anyway?"

"I wish I knew." Kaylee sighed.

"I've only known her a few weeks, but she seems on the up and up."

"I thought so too. So maybe the camera has nothing to do with the crime. But we can both agree she's crazy about Arnold, right?"

"Yeah. The question is, how crazy?"

11

Saturdays were busy at The Flower Patch, between setting up for special events and juggling the influx of orders from customers running errands on their days off. Today Kaylee was grateful for the distraction. It didn't give her time to dwell on the mystery surrounding Amber's death, particularly Wilma's potential connection.

But when she saw Sheriff Maddox pull up in front of Death by Chocolate next door in the early afternoon, her curiosity about what, if anything, he'd learned since the previous night got the better of her. "Hey, Mary, I'm going to slip next door to pick up a coffee and muffin. You want something?"

Mary glanced out the front window with a knowing smile. "Yeah, I want to hear all about what you find out as soon as you come back."

Unfortunately, a group of tourists chose that moment to wander in and browse, followed almost immediately by two more chattering groups. Kaylee couldn't abandon Mary in the middle of a rush, so she dutifully welcomed each customer and asked how she might help them, and by the time she finished boxing up a collection of DeeDee's soaps and lotions for the last customer, Sheriff Maddox's cruiser was gone.

"Go over anyway," Mary said. "Jessica might've gotten something out of him."

"I doubt it. I haven't had a chance to tell her about last night's developments yet."

The bell above the door jingled again and Aida Friedman strolled in.

"You're a couple of days early for a fresh bouquet of carnations," Mary said.

Aida waved off the teasing with a twinkle in her eye. "Not buying for the office today. I have a birthday party for my friend's grandmother to go to tonight and I thought I'd get her a potted plant. Something that doesn't need much light, because her apartment has north-facing windows."

"No problem." Kaylee came around the counter to show her the best options. "North-facing windows actually provide the most consistent light levels, so they are great locations for a lot of plants, especially foliage-based ones like the *Aspidistra elatior.*"

Aida gave her a blank look.

Kaylee pointed to the one she had in the corner. "It's also known as the cast iron plant because it's so hardy."

Aida wiggled her nose as if uninspired by the option. "I was kind of hoping for something with more color."

"Anything in the *Begoniaceae* family would do great."

Aida turned to Mary. "Translation?"

Mary laughed. "She means begonias. We have a pot over here that just started flowering."

Aida frowned at it as if she couldn't make up her mind if she liked it or not.

"Many varieties of orchids also do well in north windows," Kaylee suggested, guiding her to their selection.

Aida grinned. "Yes! That will be perfect. I'll take the pink one. Pink is her favorite color."

As Kaylee rang up the purchase, she casually asked Aida if she'd heard whether Eddie had made any headway on tracking down information on Amber's clients.

"Her brother took the ferry back to Seattle and let himself into her apartment, where he found the business card of an insurance company that occasionally hires her to investigate potential fraud cases. The card had an appointment date and everything. But the sheriff has no idea if that's who hired her for her current case," Aida said.

"The company wouldn't tell him?"

"The person who answered the number on the card said that department doesn't have staff in on the weekends, and apparently that department is pretty hush-hush. The employees who take claims calls or provide quotes had no clue who Amber was or who would know what she was doing for the company. So it'll likely be Tuesday before Eddie can find out."

"Amber's brother didn't find any of his sister's notes on her cases? Names of the people she was investigating?"

"That's the other crazy thing. He said it should have all been on her computer, but her hard drive appeared to have been wiped."

"Seriously? Was the place broken into?"

"Not that he could tell. He thinks it was done remotely. He said she had her computer synced to her phone, so it's possible she did it herself."

Kaylee shook her head. "Or whoever took her phone and threw it into the housekeeper's trash bag wiped it."

"Wow," Mary said, "he'd have to have some impressive hacking skills to break into her phone."

"Unless he forced her to give up her passwords," Kaylee said.

"Are you talking about Wilma?" DeeDee asked, joining them at the counter.

Kaylee had been so engrossed in what Aida was saying that she hadn't even noticed DeeDee come in. But at the mention of Wilma's name, Kaylee's curiosity piqued. "Why would you think that?"

DeeDee slapped her smartphone onto the counter. "My phone and every device synced to it has been hijacked and held for ransom. The hacker says if I don't pay $2,000 within the next twenty-four hours everything will be wiped out. We're talking all my business records!"

"No way," Mary said. "People can do that?"

"Oh yeah," Aida said. "Hackers gain control of your device by getting you to click on a link or attachment they send you in an e-mail, usually one masquerading as a message from a friend. Once you click, they can get into your system, where they can steal data or render it inaccessible to you."

DeeDee groaned. "That's exactly what happened. I got an e-mail from Wilma, saying her laptop was stolen out of her car, and she needed me to resend her all the photographs from my camera for her presentation. She said she'd set up an online portal, and I simply had to click the link."

"And you would've had no reason to be suspicious of it," Kaylee said sympathetically.

"Right, so of course I clicked it." DeeDee rolled her eyes. "At first nothing happened. So I waited, thinking it would open a new page, but then my screen went blank and I figured my Internet was down. We've had problems with our router in the shop. Anyway, I decided to text Wilma to let her know I got her message and would send the photos as soon as I could. But as soon as I unlocked my phone, the Internet browser opened and said my devices were being held for ransom."

"That's scary," Mary said.

"Yeah, and now I don't even have Wilma's phone number to call her, because it's on my phone, which I can't use!"

"I could try calling her," Kaylee said, "but let's do it from the landline, in case her phone has been hijacked too and the hacker can somehow infect whoever calls her."

Aida pulled out her phone. "I'll let the sheriff know what's going on. You might not be the only one the hacker has targeted. He might want to let others know to be more careful."

"Yeah," DeeDee said glumly, "especially to anyone else who's e-mailed Wilma photos. If we can't reach her, I was hoping one of you would be willing to run over to the school and let her and the others know. Maybe leave a message at the Turtle Cove Inn too, so people will get it when they return to their rooms. Andy is taking the computer to Get Wired to see if Keith can break into it. Paying the ransom would blow our budget with no guarantee we'd get our privacy back." She shuddered. "I hate to think what they're already doing with the information. I better call my bank and credit card company."

Kaylee hung up the telephone receiver. "Wilma's not answering her phone. You go on and meet Andy and contact the bank and such. I'll find Wilma and make sure everyone who has sent her photos is told not to open any e-mails from her."

"Thanks." DeeDee squeezed Kaylee's arm, then scooped up her phone. "I hope no one else made the same mistake I did. What a mess."

Kaylee left Bear with Mary at the shop and drove over to the high school to find Wilma. Cheers rose from the baseball diamond where a dozen brave alumni had accepted the challenge of a game with the upcoming senior class. Kaylee spotted Mr. Fletcher coaching a runner on third base. Ewan was edging off first as if he might try to steal second. Nina bounced up and down on the sidelines, loudly cheering Reggie, who was up to bat.

Kaylee scanned the bench and then the bleachers, trying to find Wilma.

Reese joined her. "I thought you had to be in the shop all day?"

"I thought so too, but circumstances intervened." She explained what happened to DeeDee's computer.

Reese winced. "That sounds like too much of a coincidence to not be somehow connected to the theft of Amber's camera."

"You're right." She shook her head, mystified she hadn't

made the connection herself. "I was so focused on ensuring no one else fell prey to DeeDee's hacker I didn't think about why he targeted her in particular."

Reese glanced toward the bleachers. "We need to find out if anyone else who sent Wilma photos has been targeted."

"Wilma can tell us who to ask." He pointed to Wilma, who was chatting with Arnold by the players' bench.

Reggie whacked the ball clear out of the field to shouts of "Home run!" Runners jogged the bases, gloating as the scorekeeper tallied three more runs in the alumni's favor on the scoreboard.

Reese stopped short of the dugout until the hubbub died down. "She'll want to make an announcement about this before the next inning. Hopefully with all the activities that have been going on, most people haven't had a chance to check their e-mails."

As a new batter walked to the mound, Kaylee and Reese tugged Wilma aside and filled her in on the situation.

"That's terrible!" she exclaimed. "I didn't send the e-mail, I swear. I wouldn't have any idea how to hack someone's devices like that. But my laptop was stolen last night from my car. I haven't reported it to the police yet." Wilma pulled her phone from her pocket.

"I wouldn't do anything on there that requires the Internet right now," Kaylee cautioned her.

"Good point." Wilma huffed out a frustrated sigh and stuffed the phone back in her pocket.

"Who knew you'd need the photos again?" Reese asked.

"I lamented to everyone who was still around last night about the work I'd have to do compiling the pictures all over again. But I didn't say anything about resending them. I should still have the e-mails everyone sent with the photos in the first place. I can access my account from another computer and get the photos again that way."

"You should make an announcement right now," Reese advised, "tell them they shouldn't click any links in e-mails from you."

Reggie sprang from the bench and slapped a baseball glove into Wilma's hand. "C'mon, we need you at shortstop."

"Wait, I need to make an announcement first. Actually, you know lots of stuff about computers, right, since you have that tech business? Could you help DeeDee regain control of her computer?"

"Was she hacked and ransomed?"

"Yeah."

"I could take a look, but not right now. These pups are itching to whip us. We need to keep them on the run."

"No, I didn't mean this very minute."

"Batter up!" the umpire shouted.

"They're waiting on us." Reggie, who was pitching, jogged back to the mound.

Wilma headed toward the ump, but before she reached him, Reggie threw his first pitch.

"Steee-rike," the umpire called.

"Hold on a second." Wilma signed a *T* with her hands. "Time-out."

"Game's in play," the ump said.

"I need to make an important announcement."

The other team jeered about the alumni getting cold feet.

"Can't it wait?" Reggie wound up his next pitch.

"No," Wilma said. "I'll only take a second." She gave the announcement, then trotted to her position at shortstop.

"I'm afraid no one heard that over the other team's teasing," Kaylee said to Reese.

"I'll spread the word among the spectators in the bleachers.

At this point, they're the only ones who might take the time to read e-mails. You can head back to the shop if you need to."

"Thanks."

Kaylee returned to the high school in the late afternoon to set out the arrangements she and Mary had put together for the tables. Wilma had opted to hold the dinner and dance in the school's auditorium just as their senior prom had been.

Jessica was there too, setting out the special treats she'd made. "What do you think?" she asked, stepping back to study the setup.

Everything was flower-themed, from the watering cans that doubled as water pitchers to the clay pots that would be used for pretzels and chips. Jessica had made flower-shaped chocolates, cookies, and brownies, and even decorated the tops of cupcakes with edible flowers.

"I love it," Kaylee said. "I hear they'll also have herbal teas and flower-shaped pizzas for a late-night snack."

"What's this?" Jessica asked, spotting the lone table Kaylee had filled with a selection of vases containing long-stemmed flowers from *Bellis perennis* to *Rosa alba*, or English daisy to white rose.

Kaylee moved a couple of the flowers in one vase around, then propped up the instructions sign. "We're inviting guests to share a flower with a friend or loved one. Then later we'll fill them in on the meaning of their choice."

Jessica laughed. "That sounds as if it could be dangerous. I hope none of these flowers mean anything bad. It would not go over well if a husband gave the wrong one to his wife."

"It'll be fine." Kaylee grinned. "Mary tried to sneak in some *Tagetes patula*, but I only included safe flowers."

"I know that one. Marigolds, right?"

"Very good."

"What do they mean?"

"Jealousy."

"I could think of a number of people those might not go over well with," Jessica said. "Which one should I tell Reese to give you?"

Kaylee rolled her eyes. "Tonight is for alumni and their significant others only."

"I'm sure Wilma will let the workers in on the fun. Reese volunteered to help us, you know?" Jessica fingered the petals of a red rose. "I assume this one means love."

"No, it means passion. And don't you go bullying anyone into giving anyone else a flower of any kind. We need to be focused on listening and watching for clues. Everyone will be heading home in less than forty-eight hours. This could be our last chance to catch the killer."

"You're no fun." Jessica returned her attention to arranging the delicacies she'd brought. "Have you spoken to DeeDee since this morning? I heard one of the alumni is a tech genius and was going to see if he could free DeeDee's computer without paying the ransom?"

"That's right. I sure hope Reggie can recover the data for DeeDee's sake."

"It's a shame they lost the slide show Wilma was working on. I have no idea how she's going to get it done in time now. Oh, and when the sheriff was in the bakery a little while ago, he said four others reported getting the e-mail, but by the time they saw it they knew not to click the link, so their systems weren't compromised."

"That's good at least. Did you ask him if he had any leads on who Amber might have been here to investigate?" Aida had said it would be Tuesday, but surely law enforcement had ways of finding out who Amber's contact at the insurance company would have been and what the person's home number was.

"I did." Jessica rearranged the brownies. "He's got nothing. He stopped in three times today for a coffee and chocolate, and that was only before I left. He loves his chocolate, but you know he's worried about a case when he comes in that often. Apparently not a single alum has admitted to making a recent insurance claim or to being on the pain med found in Amber's system, so it would seem that her quarry was a resident or maybe someone vacationing here."

Kaylee frowned. "Or someone is lying."

12

"What do you know about Phil?" Kaylee asked Arnold as she poured him a punch refill. She'd noticed Phil favoring his right leg as he arrived, but since then, he'd been rubbing his left knee almost every time she saw him.

Arnold glanced at Phil sitting at the nearby table, then at Cheryl, laughing as she stood among a group by the yearbook display.

It had seemed natural that Cheryl would circulate around the room since the attendees were her former classmates not Phil's, but now Kaylee wondered if his affinity for staying put had more to do with a disability.

Perhaps a disability he'd exaggerated to supplement that "early retirement" he'd been boasting about Thursday night. Some companies' medical insurance included some kind of long-term disability pension for employees too injured to return to work. And that seemed like exactly the kind of claim an insurance company would be hesitant to accept without further investigation.

Arnold shrugged. "I know about the same as you. Thursday was the first I'd met him. Why?"

"He's the only one in the group who seems to have a physical ailment."

"Actually, a couple of the women have had cancer scares, and Ewan had a heart attack last year."

"Really? Wow, he's young for that. But he's still working, right?"

"From the way he talked, I had the impression Ewan had his own veterinary practice, yes."

"What about the women you mentioned? Did they have to take a lot of time off work?"

Understanding seemed to finally dawn in Arnold's eyes. He lowered his voice and leaned over the punch bowl toward her. "You think Amber was investigating Phil?"

"Let's just say I think his story warrants a closer look."

Reese, with a platter of appetizers balanced on one hand—an image of the handyman she'd never expected to see—walked up and elbowed Arnold good-naturedly. "What's all this whispering?" he teased.

The pair walked off together. Arnold must have filled Reese in on her newest theory, because a while later he joined her in helping Jessica place cookies and bars on plates. "I think you might be onto something with Phil. Wasn't it his wife who came down with the hogweed rash?" he asked.

"Yes, but what's that got to do—" Kaylee pictured Amber's near brush with the same noxious weed. "Oh yes, Amber almost wandered into a patch of it when she slipped away from the alumni in the park to photograph something else that had caught her eye."

"Maybe something like Cheryl and Phil enjoying a more challenging walk than someone with his supposed condition could handle?" Reese's conspiratorial tone almost made her laugh, since it was something she'd expect from one of the Petal Pushers, not the practical Reese.

Then she had another thought and gasped. "Phil is probably really smart with computers too, because he used to be in business with Reggie, right?"

Reese's eyes brightened. "So he would know how to hijack the devices of anyone who might've taken an incriminating photo."

Kaylee's heart pounded double time at the realization Amber's murderer might be sitting twenty feet away from them.

"The sheriff should be able to phone Phil's boss to find out if he really retired or is actually off on disability," Jessica chimed in.

Kaylee frowned, noticing a glitch in their theory. "Didn't Phil say he started his own company after he ended his partnership with Reggie?"

"Yes," Reese said, loading the plate he was working on with too many brownies and not enough cookies. "But Arnold told me that Phil sold it eight months ago on the condition he'd stay on as a consulting development engineer until their newest product launched."

"Huh." Kaylee plucked a few brownies off Reese's plate and added them to the one she was working on. "Kind of makes you wonder what's going on with the project." She passed Reese the cookie platter. "Here, finish filling your plate with these. I'm going to call the sheriff." Kaylee walked out into the hall to search for a private place where she could make the call in peace, when movement in the parking lot caught her eye—Dave, and was that Ginger, weaving between cars?

Ginger's bodyguard glanced about as they headed toward the door.

Kaylee scanned the lot but couldn't see anyone following them. She held open the door for them. "Are you hiding from someone?"

Ginger huffed out a frustrated breath as she shed the unbecoming sun hat and cape that had effectively disguised her appearance. "I should have gone home. Changing vehicles isn't going to do any good if the jerk saw us arrive."

"Jocko?" Kaylee glanced out the window and realized the red Maserati the pair had driven earlier was nowhere in sight.

"No," Ginger said in a snooty tone. "Paparazzi I can handle."

Dave gave Kaylee an apologetic expression, then reassured Ginger. "He wouldn't have paid any attention to a couple arriving in a Ford Escape."

Deducing that Dave was referring to Ginger's stalker, Kaylee added, "That's true. There must be at least half a dozen of those vehicles in the lot. I drive one myself."

Ginger sniffed and flounced off toward the gymnasium entrance with Dave in her wake.

Deciding this was as private an alcove as she would get for now, Kaylee dialed Sheriff Maddox.

"Appreciate the tip," the sheriff said after hearing her theory. "I'll track down the new owner of Phil's company and see what he has to say about him."

Returning to the auditorium, Kaylee spied Phil quietly watching the three guests on the opposite side of the round table chatting. No one sat on either side of him. The moment might never be more opportune.

Kaylee summoned her courage. By Monday, Phil and his wife would be back on the mainland, and any evidence the sheriff might have recovered from his hotel room or car would be long gone with him. Kaylee zigzagged through the tables and slipped into the seat beside Phil.

He seemed surprised by her appearance. Thinking fast, she asked, "How's Cheryl's hogweed rash?"

"It's not slowing her down any." Chuckling, he jutted his chin in her direction. "She's always been the social butterfly of the house."

"I couldn't help but notice when you walked in that you seem to have a sore leg. I hope you didn't get that from our hike," Kaylee said.

He'd been rubbing his thigh and abruptly stopped. "No. I hurt it in a car accident a while back. Both legs, actually, though one's worse than the other. They act up now and again."

"Do you have something you can take for it?" When he seemed reluctant to answer, she added, "I have some over-the-counter stuff in my purse if you need it."

"Thanks, but I'm fine." His cheeks reddened. "I'm actually wearing a pain patch."

Her throat thickened. "Oh yeah? I've never seen those. What kind of painkiller is in them?" she asked as casually as she could manage. According to Arnold, people with no opioid tolerance had overdosed from exposure to discarded patches, and here was Phil in possession of one. And he had apparently lied to the sheriff about it, since none of the alumni—and Kaylee took that to include their spouses—had admitted to having any prescription pain medicine. So why admit having it to her? Had he slipped up?

Phil named a product Kaylee recognized as a generic version of the pain medicine found in Amber's blood.

"Everything okay?" Cheryl asked from behind her, making Kaylee jump and send a water glass crashing to the floor.

Reese rushed over with a dustpan and broom.

Kaylee's heart was pounding so hard, she wasn't sure she could continue the conversation without giving away her suspicions. From the look Cheryl shot her, Kaylee had the uncomfortable feeling the woman had overheard her husband's admission and knew exactly what Kaylee was thinking. Kaylee rose on wobbly legs and offered an equally wobbly smile. "Have a great evening."

Reese quickly swept up the broken glass and followed her back to the food prep area. "Are you all right? You went white as a sheet."

Kaylee told him what Phil had divulged and Reese immediately called the sheriff to update him. "He seems like such a nice man," Kaylee said after Reese had disconnected. "It's hard to imagine him hurting anyone. And his leg injury is pretty obvious."

"Except that a leg injury wouldn't necessarily prohibit him from sitting at a desk or lab station for eight hours. I didn't get the impression he had the kind of job that would require him to be on his feet," Reese said.

"Hmm." Kaylee surreptitiously studied Phil's dejected expression as his wife left his table again. "Perhaps his pain or maybe the medication he takes for it affects his ability to concentrate."

Reese gave her an understanding smile. "You don't have to second-guess yourself. We told the sheriff what we learned. He'll take it from there."

"I know." Kaylee fussed with a floral arrangement on a nearby table, watching Cheryl out of the corner of her eye. "But I'd feel really bad if he suffered because of a false allegation on my part."

Cheryl headed to the punch table, clutching two empty glasses. Reggie handed a glass of punch to his wife, the ladle in his other hand, then motioned toward the glasses Cheryl held. She handed one to him. Kaylee couldn't make out what they were saying, but Cheryl's tense shoulders had relaxed a little by the time Reggie finished filling the second glass and she meandered back to her husband's side.

On the pretense of adding more juice to the punch bowl, Kaylee hurried over to the table before Reggie got away from ladling duties. She wasn't sure what she hoped he'd spill information-wise, but she figured she'd never know if she didn't try. "I wanted to thank you," she said to Reggie as he held the ladle out of the way so she could fill the bowl.

"For serving punch?"

She grinned. "That too. But no, for helping my friend DeeDee with her ransomed computer systems. I haven't heard back from her this evening. Were you able to recover her data?"

"Yes, she was lucky. The hacker left a back door open that allowed me to reverse what he'd done. It's possible she lost a few files, because as I was reclaiming access, I think the hacker clued in to what I was doing and tried a last-ditch Hail Mary pass to stop me."

"Hail Mary pass?" Kaylee asked.

Reggie laughed. "Sorry, football term. Who'd have thought the high school quarterback would become a computer geek, right? A Hail Mary is a long pass that has next to zero chance of success. In this case, he succeeded in corrupting a handful of folders, but your friend seemed to think that all the important ones were intact."

"Oh good. I'm so relieved to hear it. Any idea who would do something like this?"

Reggie's gaze shifted to a point past her shoulder—the direction in which Phil sat. "There are a lot of guys out there who could do it. The Russians in particular are notorious for this stuff."

"But don't you think it'd be the same person who stole Wilma's computer? I mean how else would he have gotten DeeDee's e-mail address and known the connection between them to write such a believable e-mail that she'd click the link without hesitation?"

He shrugged. "Most hackers get into other people's e-mails without physically being on their computers."

"But it seems a little too coincidental, don't you think?"

He shrugged again.

"I guess there wasn't a way to figure out where the hacker was operating from?"

"You know, I might have been able to if I'd thought of it at the time, but I was too busy chasing him back down his rathole before he did any more damage."

"So it's too late now?"

Nina returned to the punch table and slipped her arm through her husband's in a not-so-subtle hint that it was time for him to rejoin her.

Reggie offered Kaylee an apologetic expression. "Yes, sorry. But don't worry. I'm sure your friend will be fine."

Kaylee sighed, wondering if she should have summoned up the courage to ask him outright if Phil could be the hacker. She didn't miss the disconcerted glance Cheryl shot in Reggie's direction, which made Kaylee wonder if the woman was worried that Kaylee was talking to Reggie. After all, who'd know the man's computer skills better than his former business partner?

And while she was speculating, she had to add someone else to the mix. What if Reggie himself had been the hacker, then fixed it in an effort to throw them off his trail?

Hours later, Reese helped Kaylee carry the party supplies she'd brought to her vehicle. "Can you open the back hatch with your key fob?" he asked, shifting the boxes to one arm.

"It's already unlocked." Kaylee opened the passenger door and piled her load on the floor in front of the seat, then grabbed her water bottle from between the seats.

Reese's cell phone rang. "Who would be calling me at this time of night? It's not raining or anything."

Kaylee glanced at the starry sky and chuckled. As a handyman, Reese occasionally got calls from distraught homeowners with leaky roofs.

Reese arranged the boxes in the back of her vehicle so they wouldn't slide around, then dug his phone out of his jacket and glanced at the screen. He flashed Kaylee a concerned look. "It's Arnold." His friend had left the dinner dance early, much to Wilma's disappointment. And Reese had worried anew ever since about the man's emotional state. Reese's expression didn't improve as he listened to Arnold on the other end of the line. Disconnecting, Reese relayed his friend's news. "Deputies are at the hotel searching Phil and Cheryl's hotel room."

"Wow, Eddie must've gotten hold of Phil's former employer and confirmed our theory. That was fast. I'm amazed he found a judge on a Saturday night to sign the search warrant."

"With more than half the alumni, including Phil and Cheryl, heading off island after tomorrow's Hall of Fame finale, he probably convinced the judge time was of the essence."

Kaylee took a long swig from her water bottle. "I wish I could be a fly on the wall in that room." She grimaced at how warm and nasty her water had gotten sitting in her vehicle all evening, despite it being in an insulated bottle.

"I'm sure we'll be able to get the juicy details out of him in the morning, especially since you gave him the lead," Reese said.

"Unless it doesn't pan out. Then he might not want to talk to me."

Reese patted her shoulder. "If Eddie managed to get a search warrant, he had to have just cause. I'm sure Phil's lie about his pain med prescription didn't help his case any."

"But if he's innocent, I hate being the snitch who put the sheriff on to him."

Reese opened her driver's door. "Go home and get some sleep. By morning, we're bound to have some answers."

Within minutes of hitting the road, Kaylee's head began to swim. She blinked hard, but the blink seemed to happen in slow motion, because as she raised her eyelids she couldn't remember the past quarter mile. She drifted over the centerline and swerved back into her lane. The streetlights multiplied, hurting her eyes.

A stop sign suddenly appeared. Make that two of them.

Why would they put two stop signs side by side?

As her mind tried to sort that out, she drove straight past them, without braking. Her eyelids felt so heavy, she struggled to keep her eyes open.

Swirling red and blue lights flashed in her rearview mirror. Attracted to the image, she fixated on it. *That's so pretty.*

The sound of the road beneath her tires changed. Her gaze swerved back to the windshield. She cranked the steering wheel and the scenery circled around her. Her stomach roiled from the dizzy feeling the racing scenery gave her. Somehow, she managed to stop the car and put it in park. She closed her eyes, her mind swimming.

The next thing she knew someone was jerking open her car door. And her vehicle sat in the middle of the road, facing a colorful police car.

She squeezed her eyes shut again, because the lights made them hurt.

"Ma'am, step out of the car please," the deputy holding her door said. "Kaylee? What's wrong?"

Somewhere in the back of her mind she knew she recognized the deputy's voice, but his name remained out of her grasp. She finally managed to wrench open her eyes, and her gaze settled on the water bottle sitting in her seat console.

"I think I've been poisoned," she whispered, and the world went black.

13

Kaylee woke to a pounding headache. And she could hear voices.

Had she forgotten to turn the radio off before she went to bed?

Bear sure wouldn't have turned it on. She wiggled her feet in search of his comforting warmth. He wasn't there.

"Kaylee?"

That sounded like Reese's voice. She tugged her sheets to her chin. What was he doing at the cottage? It was too early for fall maintenance. And why couldn't she open her eyes? Was she dreaming?

"Kaylee, honey, we're here." A warm hand squeezed her arm. "It's Mary. And Reese is here too. The deputy called me because he knew we work together, and I called Reese and the rest of the Petal Pushers. We're all praying for you. The doctor is confident he got to you in time."

Doctor? Memories of the car ride swept through her mind. Her eyes flew open and she sprang up to a sitting position, which made her head pound. She quickly collapsed back against the pillows. "I was poisoned."

"The doctors say you can expect a full recovery," Reese said gently. He and Mary sat on either side of her hospital bed. "It's good to see you awake. You gave us quite a scare."

"What happened?"

"Deputy Brooks called the hospital and told them to have a lab tech standing by. As the ambulance got you loaded, he grabbed your water bottle because he said you'd stared at it when you told him you were poisoned, and then he rushed it to the lab. A poisonous mushroom had been crushed into it."

Kaylee clasped her throat, only now registering how much it hurt, probably from being intubated. "I knew the water tasted off. I thought it simply got warm from baking in the car."

What Reese had said finally sank in.

"Someone tried to kill me," she rasped. "Why?"

"Maybe you got too close to figuring out who killed Amber," Mary said.

Kaylee stared at her, struggling to process the idea. "I did?" She turned back to Reese. "Phil did this to me?"

Reese shrugged. "Maybe."

A knock sounded at the door. Sheriff Maddox stepped into the room without waiting for an invitation, closing the door behind him. "How are you feeling?"

"I have a doozy of a headache. But I'm alive."

He grimaced. "Unfortunately we're no closer to figuring out who killed Amber or who poisoned you."

"Do you think it's the same person?" Kaylee asked.

"Unless you have an enemy you haven't told me about."

She started to shake her head but caught herself when the pain intensified. "Unless . . . Phil figured out I'm the one who tipped you off about him."

Eddie settled into another chair next to Reese. "Phil's former employer did confirm the insurance company that manages their health plan and disability claims hired Amber to investigate him. They believe he exaggerated leg issues to get out of his contractual agreement to stay on with the company until he completed a research project he'd touted as an industry game changer when he sold the company."

"And Phil figured out what Amber was up to?" Mary prodded.

Eddie sighed. "That's what we guessed, since any incriminating photographs she'd captured of him could have cost him his insurance claim—or worse, led to his being charged with fraud."

"Sounds like a strong motive," Reese said.

"That's what we thought," Eddie went on. "Problem is, the search of Phil's hotel room and rental car didn't turn up any evidence. If he took Amber's camera, he must have already dumped it and hoped she hadn't had time to send any photos to the insurance company."

"What about Wilma's stolen computer? The e-mails?" Kaylee pressed. "He must still be worried there are incriminating photos out there. Can't your tech guys dig into his computer and somehow prove he's the hacker?"

Eddie shook his head. "He didn't have a computer with him. That we could find, anyway."

"What about his pain patches?" Reese asked. "Is it really possible to make someone OD with one?"

"Absolutely. And one may or may not be missing. He said he had a spare in his suitcase, but his wife said he put that one on Friday and there were no more. He didn't seem to recall, but then he acted as if he suddenly remembered as much."

"Interesting," Mary said. "It sounds as if he's covering for her."

Kaylee nodded. "She'd have just as much to lose if he lost his insurance. Maybe more, since she still works at the company."

"Perhaps," Eddie said. "Trouble is we have no proof Amber even had compromising photos, let alone that Phil or his wife took them. Neither of them has shoes that match the prints lifted from Amber's room."

"Did you check for mushroom spores on their clothes or in their car?" Kaylee asked.

"I have a tech on it."

Kaylee frowned.

"What is it?" Mary asked.

"They had to have already collected the poisonous mushrooms before dinner—and before I even questioned Phil about his leg."

"So maybe you weren't the intended target," Mary interjected. "You said the soap star had a stalker threatening her, didn't you?"

Kaylee gasped. "Yes. And they drove a Ford Escape last night. They told me they switched vehicles to escape the guy's notice."

"Only maybe he did notice they were driving an Escape," Mary said. "But settled on yours by mistake."

Kaylee nodded. "That's possible. Ginger always seems to have a personal water bottle on hand. What if the guy saw mine between the seats and assumed it was hers?"

Eddie drew his notepad from his pocket and flipped through the pages. "Did your mechanic say what made your tire blow?"

"My tire?" Kaylee pressed her palm to her forehead, struggling to follow what that had to do with anything.

"The one you changed last night," he prompted.

"Oh. I picked up a nail somewhere. Why?"

"I'm wondering if it wasn't an accident after all."

Kaylee gulped.

"You think it was a first attempt on her life?" Reese asked. "Because she was asking questions?"

"Could be," Eddie said.

Kaylee closed her eyes and pictured the hotel's parking lot that night. She must have seen the perpetrator lurking about without realizing it. Her eyes popped open at another memory. "Cheryl and Phil were outside the hotel manager's office when I asked about key card evidence. It's possible they overheard us talking."

Eddie nodded. "I'll check the hotel's security footage for the time your car was in the lot. See if we can get some solid proof against the pair."

"She should have protection," Mary said.

"You know I don't have enough deputies to offer that," Eddie said. He met Kaylee's gaze once more. "But I did instruct the front desk and nursing staff to not give out your room number."

"No, I can't stay. Bear will—" She sat up, but her head swam so viciously, she had to lie back down.

"I'm taking care of Bear," Mary said soothingly.

"You're in no condition to leave," Eddie added. "And you should be safe here for the rest of the night."

Reese got comfortable in his chair. "I intend to make sure of it."

By morning Kaylee felt almost back to normal, much better than Reese looked after a night of sleeping pretzeled in an uncomfortable armchair. Around eight, the doctor came and declared her well enough to go home, with a warning to only eat mushrooms she bought at the grocery store.

She didn't bother to correct his misconception about how she'd been poisoned. She was too happy about being discharged. She hadn't realized how oppressive the smell of antiseptic could get. "Give me two minutes to change and then we can get out of here," Kaylee said to Reese, before slipping into the restroom.

When she emerged minutes later, the clicking of doggy toenails on the marble floor outside the door brought a grin to her lips. Bear raced into the room, decked out in his best bow tie and hauling Mary after him.

"Someone couldn't wait another minute to see you," Mary said with a grin. "I nearly had to bribe the receptionist, but Bear charmed her into letting him in, as long as I promised he would only be in your room."

Kaylee scooped Bear into her arms. "Thank you." She nuzzled his fur. "Did you miss me?"

He covered her cheek with enthusiastic kisses.

"Well, I hate to drop off a dog and run," Mary said with a

chuckle, "but Wilma asked if she could come by the shop at nine to pick up the centerpieces for the dinner cruise, since you were out of commission."

A cold chill slithered down Kaylee's spine. "How'd she know I was out of commission?"

Mary's eyes widened, clearly cluing in to the potential implication.

"Jess or DeeDee probably told her," Reese said, although Kaylee hadn't missed the twitch in his jaw.

DeeDee burst into the room with Jessica at her side. "Told who what?"

"That Kaylee was in the hospital," Mary explained.

"Yes," DeeDee said. "I told her I wasn't sure how much help we would be today with the dinner cruise, since we needed to be with Kaylee."

"I'd say we can definitely rule out Kaylee being there," Reese said.

"No! We have to go," Kaylee argued. "This could be our last chance to ferret out Amber's killer."

"How?" Reese asked. "What if he has another go at you?"

"If that's what it takes," Kaylee said quietly. "We have to stop him. Or her. Before someone else gets hurt."

Reese looked like he was about to protest, but then he smiled. "You're more than a match for any killer."

"Especially with all of us on the job too," DeeDee said. "But surely Phil or Cheryl wouldn't dare try to hurt her again. Not when they know the sheriff is watching them."

"What if it wasn't Phil or Cheryl who did this?" Reese countered.

"Whoever tried to poison me wouldn't be foolish enough to try again. They'll expect me to be extra cautious," Kaylee reasoned. "If it was Phil, he's not going to risk getting caught. If it wasn't

Phil, then the perpetrator has done a great job of framing him, so why jeopardize that? Besides, I'd feel safer with everyone else around than home alone in my cottage."

"I can't argue with that," Reese said. "If you're going, then at least let me come along to watch your back."

Kaylee grinned. "How can I refuse that offer? It'll be like being a movie star with a bodyguard of my own."

Jessica laughed "Might make Ginger jealous."

Three hours later, Kaylee and Reese left Bear with Mary at The Flower Patch and joined the alumni gathered on the pier waiting to board the yacht. Mr. Fletcher had joined them for the excursion and was chatting to a group of women about orchids. Kaylee was about to slide over and join the conversation when Reese jutted his chin toward the parking lot. "They're here."

Phil stood next to his rental car with the passenger door open, but Cheryl wasn't climbing out. They seemed to be arguing, but Phil must have won, because a moment later Cheryl climbed out of the car and stalked toward the pier. "It's my reunion. It should be my decision," she groused at him as they came within earshot.

"We are going on the cruise," Phil said firmly. "The lunch is already paid for. And leaving now would only make me seem guilty."

Cheryl stopped mere feet away from where Reese and Kaylee stood and lowered her voice. "They're going to talk. Or whisper behind our backs."

"Let them. I have nothing to hide. I'm legitimately disabled and I deserve the payments I'm receiving. If you hadn't begged me to put a positive spin on the situation and tell your former classmates I retired early, everyone would already know that. And if Amber had truly been paying attention, she would have come to the same conclusion."

Cheryl adjusted the brim of her floppy sun hat. "It's not only that. I shouldn't be out in the sun either. The doctor said so. I could have another reaction."

"There are tables inside. You don't have to sit on deck." Phil clasped her arm and tugged her toward the end of the line waiting to board. "Come on. Everything will be fine."

The line started moving and guests already aboard the yacht grew quiet and gave Phil and Cheryl a wide berth when the pair moved through the cabin. Cheryl squirmed under the stares, but Phil held his head high and moved steadily toward a window seat in the dining area.

"Knock it off, guys," Reggie said loudly. "The only thing Phil and Cheryl are guilty of is being the victims of a bad hunch on the sheriff's part."

People started chatting again after the reproof, but not to Phil and Cheryl. A woman near Kaylee muttered, "He wasn't exactly honest about his early retirement."

Reggie slung an arm across the woman's shoulders and said, "A man's ego is a fragile thing. The sheriff hasn't arrested them. The least we can do is give them the benefit of the doubt."

The man's fair-mindedness and rapport with the group was impressive. It wasn't hard to see why he'd continued to be as successful in business as he'd been in winning the high school's popularity contest. He walked over to where Phil and Cheryl had taken seats and squeezed Cheryl's shoulder, then shook Phil's hand. "Glad you joined us. The rest will come around. You'll see."

It was Phil's turn to squirm, apparently more uncomfortable with his ex-partner's magnanimous vote of confidence in his character than the stares of his wife's classmates. Phil rubbed his knee and said loud enough for those around him to hear, "I didn't consciously lie to the sheriff. He asked if we had a pain *pill* prescription. I never even thought about my pain patch being of interest to him."

Reggie slapped him on the back. "I can see how that would happen. Don't beat yourself up over it."

After Reggie moved away from their table, others eventually happened by to assure Phil and Cheryl of their belief in Phil's innocence. Kaylee couldn't afford to keep such an open mind, but she scrutinized the other passengers for any sign of interest in her presence.

Ewan joined her. "Can I get you a drink?"

"No thanks," she said.

"You feeling seasick?"

"Do I look that bad?"

Ewan chuckled. "You are a little peaked."

"Hmm." Kaylee grimaced. "I had a rough night."

"Oh? Something you ate?"

"You could say that."

"Some animals are notorious for that. The slightest change in diet can set them off. Of course it doesn't help that their owners don't always know what's bad for them. I had one client who made his German shepherd horribly sick by feeding him leftover onion-laden gravy on his dry dog food. Had no idea onions are toxic to dogs."

Given Reggie and Phil's earlier conversation, Kaylee couldn't resist saying, "I guess you prescribe a fair amount of pain medication to the pet patients you see, don't you?"

"Yes."

She was surprised by the unabashed admission. "Would it be possible to cause someone to OD using a pain patch?" She already knew the answer to that, but she wanted to hear what Ewan had to say.

"For sure. That's why I will rarely send a pet home with one, and definitely won't if there are children in the home. Someone not used to opiates could easily absorb a lethal dose through the skin if they punctured the gel on the patch. And if I do prescribe one, I always have clients return to my office to have their pets' patches removed and disposed of appropriately."

It occurred to Kaylee that Ewan had left the restaurant soon after Amber had, giving him opportunity as well as know-how. But not a hint of anxiety had colored his response, which meant he was innocent, right?

Or it could mean he's guilty and completely without a conscience.

14

The group cruised around the outer islands for more than an hour. The tour guide recited details about the area and its marine life along the way, but most of the alumni seemed to be only half listening, between chatting with old classmates and oohing and aahing over orca sightings, or snapping photos of sea lions and porpoises. The yacht Wilma had commissioned was even outfitted with hydrophones so they could listen to the whale calls.

A little after noon, they entered the Friday Harbor Marine Preserve. "The preserve was established in partnership with the University of Washington to protect the area from overfishing for bottom fish and invertebrates," the tour guide explained, causing several alumni to begin reminiscing over fishing stories.

The captain gave the order to lower the anchor. "We'll stop here for lunch," he declared.

"Thank goodness," Kaylee said to Reese. The water had been choppy all morning and neither her head nor her stomach was handling it as well as they normally would have if she hadn't spent the night in the hospital recovering from being poisoned.

A line quickly formed along the buffet tables laden with tempting varieties of seafood, sandwiches, and salads. Kaylee brought up the rear and longingly eyed the quickly disappearing crackers.

Ewan detoured out of the line to the port rail. "Hey, guys, you have to see this." He pointed at an eagle soaring on the wind currents. For the alumni who still lived on the island, it was a common sight that distracted them from the food line for only a moment. However, a few others gasped at the majestic creature.

One even declared it was the first time she'd ever seen an eagle.

Kaylee gingerly took advantage of the line leavers to nab the last few crackers.

Wilma, who'd been busily rearranging the table decorations, reached for the near-empty plate of stuffed mushroom caps and offered them to Kaylee.

Kaylee stifled a wince. "Uh, no thanks. I've lost my appetite for mushrooms."

Wilma ducked her head sheepishly. "Of course you have. I'm sorry. Do you want more crackers? I can ask the steward if they have more."

"That would be great. Thank you," Kaylee said. "My stomach is still a bit off."

Reese squeezed her shoulder.

"You don't like mushrooms?" Dave, Ginger's bodyguard asked, reaching past Kaylee to help himself to the last mushroom cap.

"Had a nasty experience with some bad ones recently."

"Did you?" He popped the cap into his mouth. "That can be deadly. My parents used to collect mushrooms from the fields when I was a kid. Then someone in our town died from eating the wrong kind."

Kaylee stifled a shudder and quipped, "I hope they chose to do their hunting and gathering in the grocery store after that."

Dave laughed. "You bet. It would have been dumb to take any more chances."

As he moved on to the bar at the end of the table and asked for a refill of Ginger's drink, Reese moved a little closer to Kaylee. "You feeling all right?"

"Sure." She added a couple of carrot sticks to her plate and trailed Reese back to their table. Her gaze collided with Cheryl's. The woman abruptly returned her attention to her food. "Did you see that?" Kaylee asked Reese in a low voice.

He nodded.

"You think she's surprised to see me still vertical?" Kaylee asked. The sheriff's search of Phil and Cheryl's hotel room might have been a bust, but Kaylee still didn't trust the couple.

Reese slid across the bench seat opposite her. "Or she suspects you of tipping off the sheriff about her husband's pain prescription."

"Exactly." Kaylee leaned over the table and lowered her voice. "Which gave her motive to put an end to my tips. On the other hand, Eddie didn't search their room until after they left the dance last night, so how could she have known to poison me?"

"Ginger's bodyguard seemed to know a lot about mushrooms," Reese noted.

"Seriously? He has no motive." Kaylee nibbled a cracker.

Reese shrugged. "Amber's missing camera, Wilma's stolen laptop, and the computer hack all suggest someone wants to ensure incriminating photos don't see the light of day. And Ginger sure seems hypersensitive about being photographed."

"Because she's a soap star who wants some privacy."

"Maybe." He swirled a meatball around in the sauce on his plate. "But I suspect she's on the island for more than the reunion."

"Why do you say that?"

"Yesterday, I spotted them walking out of a house for sale on my street."

"Window-shopping to kill time before the next reunion event?"

"Maybe. But DeeDee saw them at that real estate office, and the reporter who wrote the tabloid article—Jocko—might have seen something similar."

Wilma happened toward them at that moment and Kaylee waved her over to their table. "In all the photos you've seen from the reunion, did you see any of Ginger checking out properties for sale?"

"You know you shouldn't believe everything you read in the tabloids."

Reese chuckled.

"So that's a no?" Kaylee asked.

"No, not that I recall. Why?"

"Just curious. Thanks."

Wilma moved on, and Kaylee and Reese returned to eating.

Two twittering women at a nearby table snagged Kaylee's attention. Ewan sat opposite them.

"Did you happen to notice anything odd between Amber and Ewan the first night?" Kaylee asked Reese.

He lifted his mug of coffee to his lips and casually followed her gaze. "What are you thinking?"

She shrugged. "He seemed overly interested in how I was feeling earlier and instantly guessed it was something I ate. And he has access to opiates. And he left the restaurant soon after Amber the other night. And he was at last night's dance."

"Which is true of three-quarters of the alumni on board," Reese said softly. "I didn't get the sense he knew Amber before he joined our table. But if she was killed because of taking an incriminating photo, I guess he didn't need to."

"That's another thing. He was the one who suggested that was the killer's motive in the first place. Said it could have been a cheating husband or something."

Reese glanced over his shoulder once more, but Ewan had already left the table.

The yacht's motor kicked in and the captain announced he was pulling up anchor. As guests finished their desserts, the yacht began a slow turn away from the serenity of the sheltered cove. The wind had begun to pick up significantly in the time it'd taken them to eat lunch. "Looks as though we'll be in for a rougher ride back to Orcas Island," the captain informed them.

Groans echoed through the cabin.

Arnold and Wilma headed their way. The boat pitched and Wilma stumbled.

Arnold caught her by the arm and held it until they reached the table.

"I guess the lunchtime cruise wasn't such a good idea," Wilma said to them.

"Nonsense," Arnold reassured her. Kaylee thought his eyes seemed a little brighter than she'd seen them since Amber's death. "The cruise was a perfect idea. It's not your fault the weather didn't cooperate."

"I'm having a lovely time anyway," Kaylee added. "You've done a fantastic job with this entire reunion."

Wilma glowed at the affirmation. "We were going to go out on deck and watch for whales," she said. "Do you two want to join us?"

"That sounds great," Reese said, then caught Kaylee's warning expression. "But I think Kaylee should rest for a bit. I'll keep her company, but you guys go ahead and enjoy those whales."

"I hope you feel better soon," Wilma told her, but Kaylee got the impression that she wasn't even a little bit disappointed to have Arnold all to herself. They walked away.

"Do you think he realizes how much Wilma adores him?" Kaylee asked Reese.

"I hope so. The last thing I want to see him do is swear off dating after the way Amber manipulated him. Once he heard she was a PI, he went from feeling guilt-ridden to something even worse—feeling useless, as if she hadn't had feelings for him because he wasn't worth having feelings for."

"That's so sad, especially when Amber isn't here to defend herself. I know her brother thinks she was using Arnold as a cover for her investigation, but for all we know, she may have honestly liked him."

Reese's expression told her he doubted it.

Remembering how little attention Amber had shown Arnold in the time they were together, Kaylee doubted it herself. Hopefully Arnold would heal and allow himself to move on.

Ewan ambled up to their table and set a cloudy pink drink in front of Kaylee. "I noticed you weren't eating much at lunch, so I asked the bartender to mix this drink for you. Works wonders at settling the stomach."

"Oh. Thank you. Um, what's in it?" Kaylee asked, exchanging a glance with Reese.

Ewan rattled off a list of innocuous ingredients.

Kaylee nodded. "I appreciate you thinking of me." She handed the drink back to him. "But I'm afraid grapefruit juice has never agreed with me."

"Right, um, okay."

Reese snagged it out of his hand. "I'll try it. Sounds intriguing."

Ewan grinned. "Enjoy."

"Are you nuts?" Kaylee hissed once the man was out of earshot. "That could be poisoned."

"Exactly," Reese said. "And we wouldn't have been able to prove it if we let him dump it down the sink, would we?"

She should have thought of that. "Good thinking."

"Maybe. Except he wouldn't have believed he could hand over a poisoned drink so openly and not get caught."

"So I'm being paranoid?"

"Maybe a little." Reese put the drink to his lips and pretended to sip. At least she hoped he was pretending. He winked, but then his gaze shifted to something behind her.

The back of Kaylee's neck prickled. "Is he watching us?"

"Phil is."

Kaylee shuddered. "Sitting here isn't getting us any closer

to figuring out who killed Amber or poisoned me. I think we should ask each alumnus to show us any pictures they've taken this weekend. If our theory about all of this being connected to an incriminating photo is correct, then that should make our guy real nervous."

Reese heaved a weighty sigh. "Any chance I can convince you to put a life jacket on before we start? You know, in case our nervous guy accidentally knocks you overboard."

Kaylee gaped at him, and it took her a few swallows before she could get an answer out of her clogged throat. "We'll only ask people who are inside."

"Good plan. Let me get an empty bottle from the galley first so I can save a sample of this drink. I'll be right back."

A female alumna Kaylee hadn't yet met immediately claimed his seat. "You're the florist, right?"

"Yes."

"I had to tell you how much I love the decorations you had at the dance last night. They were so cute, but not sappy, you know?"

"Thank you," Kaylee said with a smile.

"My daughter's getting married on the mainland soon. I was wondering if you had any ideas or tips for that. Here's the venue." She introduced herself as Carla and pulled out her phone and showed Kaylee a few photos. "I think it's a little sparse, but she insists that she wants a minimalistic wedding. What does that even mean?"

Kaylee smiled. "It's a trend at the moment. Kind of a less-is-more approach. You stick with simple shapes and few colors, but you make them contrast for high visual impact. Let me show you." She found some photos on her own phone of another wedding she'd recently done and showed them to the woman.

"That's so pretty! So what would you do for this space?"

"I would do mostly greenery, with maybe a few roses or lilies in the main wedding color. I think fairy lights would be gorgeous in the rafters here too, but I wouldn't do much more than that."

"Thanks. I think I just needed someone to explain what it meant, you know?"

When the woman backed out of the close-ups of the wedding venue and into her gallery page, Kaylee couldn't help noticing that Carla also had several photos from the weekend, more of decorations than of people, but sometimes it was the wallflowers one needed to worry about.

"I'm sorry, but do you mind if I look at the photos you've taken this weekend? I love seeing things from someone else's perspective."

"Sure. Here," she said, handing it over.

Neither Phil nor Ginger appeared in any of the pictures. Nor Ewan either, for that matter.

"It's too bad Wilma's computer got hacked or she could show the slide show she'd been working on of all the photos everyone e-mailed her," the alumna went on. "Maybe we could set up a private group where we could share our pictures online and view them that way."

"That's a great idea."

"What's a great idea?" Reese asked, returning to the table.

"A shared photo album online," Kaylee explained, handing the phone back.

"I can do it right now. It won't take long." The woman tapped away on the screen of her smartphone. A few minutes later she presented Kaylee with the result. "There. What do you think?"

"Perfect." Kaylee pulled out her own phone to navigate to the page Carla had created.

"The password is 'reunion25.'"

Kaylee typed it in and the page loaded, fully functional. "Perfect. We'll help spread the word."

"Thanks. And thanks for your advice about the wedding. I want my little girl's day to be perfect."

"Of course," Kaylee said with a smile.

Carla went back to visiting with her classmates as Kaylee and Reese moved on to the next table to tell others about the online scrapbook. Hopefully anyone with pictures on their phone would upload them immediately so she could see as many photos as possible before Amber's attacker caught on and took countermeasures.

At DeeDee's table, Kaylee explained what was going on, then asked her friend, "Can we access the photos from your camera, so they can be added too?"

"No. They were in one of the folders the stupid hacker corrupted. Reggie couldn't recover them."

Reggie, sitting at the next table, glanced their way at the mention of his name.

Kaylee lowered her voice. "Do you remember any photos someone might consider incriminating?"

"There were some of Ginger. She seems to think any photo of her is a bad thing."

"They would give away where she is if the background is identifiable," Reese pointed out.

Dave, who'd clearly been eavesdropping, joined them. "It doesn't even matter if the background is generic. Nowadays, your average Joe or Jane can access the metadata on the photo file and see the GPS location where it was taken. Not that anyone has to bother half the time, considering everyone and their grandmother posts their photos publicly on their social media pages with a 'guess who I ran into in Turtle Cove' caption."

"I guess that makes your job even tougher," Reese said.

"It sure doesn't help."

"Where's Ginger now?" Kaylee asked.

"The ladies' room. These waves are killing her, and she isn't feeling well enough to socialize."

Kaylee glanced from the now cleared table where Ginger and Dave had been sitting to the door of the restroom. "When did she start feeling sick?"

"As soon as we started moving again after lunch."

"I'll go check on her," Kaylee said. She had to support herself by gripping the backs of the booth seats along the way. The ride was rough, but Kaylee couldn't help comparing Ginger's state to how she'd felt last night, and of the possibility her SUV and water bottle had been mistaken for Ginger's.

What if someone wanted Ginger to think she was only seasick—until it was too late?

15

Kaylee tapped on the door of the only occupied stall in the ladies' room. "Ginger? What's wrong?"

A moan drifted out. "Go away."

"Could it have been something you ate?" Kaylee pressed.

Ginger's stall door snapped open. Her complexion was ashen, and her eyes seemed almost sunken. "Was the shrimp bad?"

The question momentarily threw Kaylee. "I don't think so. No one else seems to be sick from the food. You think that's what it was? The water is pretty choppy. My stomach felt a little queasy already on the trip into the harbor."

"This isn't just a woozy, nauseated feeling." She sank to the floor, clutching her stomach. "My stomach is cramping horribly. But I've never been seasick before, so I don't know if this is normal or not."

"Did anything you eat or drink taste odd?"

"I only had shrimp and a couple of drinks. Everything tasted fine." Ginger squeezed her eyes shut, apparently bracing against a fresh wave of pain. Perspiration beaded on her forehead and lips. She shoved her hand into her pocket and pulled out a tissue she pressed to her lips. A slip of paper floated to the floor.

Kaylee retrieved it and held it out to her.

When she saw it, Ginger's eyes widened and her face went even whiter. "He's here."

"Who's here?" Kaylee read the note Ginger was staring at in horror.

Are you sure you can trust your bodyguard to protect you?

"Do you think your stalker wrote this?" Kaylee asked.

"Who else?" Ginger squeezed her eyes shut and tears leaked from the corners. Tremors overtook her body. "He's poisoned me. He's poisoned me."

"I'll get Dave and tell the captain to rush us to the closest hospital."

Reese and Dave were both hovering outside the door. Kaylee showed them the note and Dave stormed into the restroom.

"We'll talk to the captain," Kaylee called after him.

Kaylee and Reese rushed to the bridge and apprised the captain of Ginger's condition.

"We should be back to Orcas Island within the hour," he said sympathetically, but clearly doubting Ginger had anything worse than a case of seasickness.

"She may not have an hour!" Kaylee snapped.

The captain turned a doubtful frown to Reese. "From food poisoning?"

"We believe someone deliberately put poison in her food." Reese showed him the note.

The captain's eyes widened and he immediately began to turn his vessel. "The closest medical facility is back at Friday Harbor." He glanced at the first mate. "Notify the coast guard. Tell them we'll need an ambulance standing by." He ramped up the speed. "ETA 15 minutes. Tell them we need the police too. No one besides the victim and her bodyguard will be allowed to leave the ship until the authorities allow it."

Some of the tension drained from Kaylee's muscles. "We should go back to the others," she said to Reese, eager to watch for suspicious behavior among the passengers and crew.

The captain announced over the intercom that they needed to head back to Friday Harbor for a medical emergency.

A shrill-voiced woman, who must have guessed Ginger's illness, dumped what was left of her dessert and drink over the side of the ship. Others began to follow suit.

"Stop!" Kaylee shouted. "If food's been contaminated, the police will want to test it. Besides, dumping it could be dangerous for the wildlife here." She scanned the faces of the group, looking for signs of guilt.

Arnold rushed toward Reese with Wilma on his heels. "Is this connected to the attack on Amber?"

"We don't know," Kaylee said. "Ginger has been dodging a stalker for some time."

Arnold made the connection. "So this stalker could have mistaken Amber for Ginger?"

"The sheriff has been considering that possibility," Kaylee admitted.

Arnold searched Kaylee's gaze. "But you don't think that's what happened?"

Kaylee sighed. "I don't know what to think. Nothing makes complete sense."

The crew covered the buffet tables with plastic sheets to preserve potential evidence. The atmosphere on the ship grew subdued as everyone took their seats and waited for the ship to dock at Friday Harbor.

As soon as the vessel was secured at the dock, investigators boarded, along with paramedics. Ginger and Dave were allowed to leave, but everyone else was asked to stay. The captain directed the lead investigator, Detective Booker, to Kaylee, who filled him in on the events of the past couple of days that might be connected.

"Verify that every person aboard is supposed to be here," Detective Booker instructed one of the deputies.

As another photographed the buffet table and collected food samples, Kaylee scrutinized the scene. "Wilma, weren't there berries on the American bittersweet vine when Mary gave it to you this morning?"

Wilma surveyed the arrangement Kaylee pointed to on the refreshment table. "Yes, red berries. Are they poisonous?"

Detective Booker came up behind them. "Are what poisonous?"

"*Celastrus scandens,*" Kaylee said. "The American bittersweet vine. Its berries would cause severe gastrointestinal upset."

"But Miss Andrews said she ingested only shrimp and a couple drinks," Detective Booker said. "How easily could the berries have been disguised in either of those?"

Kaylee shrugged.

Mr. Fletcher, standing on the other side of the table, said, "The berries have a strong flavor, but the taste would've been easy enough to overlook if they were crushed into the cocktail sauce, since it's tangy and red."

Wilma shuddered.

Kaylee noticed a deputy had already bagged and tagged the platter of shrimp and dish of sauce, but unless no one else ate shrimp, surely the tainting had to have happened directly on Ginger's plate. "It's hard to believe her bodyguard would have let anyone close enough to her food to tamper with it."

"Except he'd stopped by our table without her. Remember?" Reese said. "So he couldn't have been paying that close attention to what she was eating."

Wilma chewed on her bottom lip. "This is horrible. I never should've organized the reunion."

"Nonsense," Mr. Fletcher said. "This isn't your fault. Whoever is tormenting Ginger would have gotten to her wherever she went."

A deputy snapped a picture of the shelves behind the bar, and it occurred to Kaylee that between all the pictures everyone had been snapping of each other throughout the cruise, one might've inadvertently captured the perpetrator in the act of tainting Ginger's sauce. "We need a way to study the digital images we've collected," Kaylee whispered to Reese, "and get copies of all the ones from today's cruise we've missed."

They started making the rounds of the alumni, once more reminding everyone to upload all their photos of the weekend to the page they'd set up. Kaylee texted Mary with the link and the password and asked her to immediately download all the photos that came in.

What's going on? she texted back.

I want to have backups in case our hacker gets to the site, Kaylee texted. She added a brief explanation of what had happened.

"A few of the women couldn't get reception or didn't have a good enough data plan on their phone to upload the photos, so they texted them to my phone," Reese said to Kaylee.

"That's great. Can you upload them?" Kaylee lowered her voice. "Mary is making copies in case it gets hacked."

Reese shook his head. "My data overage charges would be through the roof." He tucked his phone into his pocket. "But don't worry. I'll keep them safe."

Kaylee's stomach turned over and she glanced around. DeeDee's ransomed computer and Kaylee's own poisoning had communicated loud and clear that whoever was behind everything wasn't above taking out anyone who got in his or her way.

Arnold joined them. "Wilma is trying to convince Detective Booker to let us sail back to Orcas Island." He glanced at his watch. "She's worried we won't return in time for the homecoming game if he holds us much longer."

"Except from his point of view," Kaylee said, "once we go, any chance of arresting the perpetrator is pretty much gone too."

Anguish contorted Arnold's face. "You'd think they'd have been able to ferret out Ginger's stalker by now."

"Before today, her stalker had only tormented her psychologically," Reese said. "The police have to consider this deadly escalation." He glanced at Kaylee and winced, no doubt thinking the escalation had in fact started with her water bottle last night, or maybe even the attack on Amber.

"It's got to be one of the crew," an alumnus chatting at the next table said, loud enough for them to overhear. "Her own classmates wouldn't do this to her."

The woman beside her said, "I'm not so sure. She broke more than a few guys' hearts and stole several girls' boyfriends. She always looked down her nose at people, and then she went and made it big in Hollywood. I could see someone carrying a grudge and seeing the reunion as an opportunity to finally get payback."

"You really think so?"

"Sure. It's not as if the person was trying to kill her. Mr. Fletcher said the detective thinks she was poisoned with a berry that'd just give her a bad stomachache, nothing lethal."

Kaylee exchanged a glance with Reese, who had also been eavesdropping on the conversation at the next table. Amber was dead. And the poison in Kaylee's water bottle had certainly had the potential to be lethal. But if either or both attacks had been the work of Ginger's stalker, why would he or she ratchet down the lethalness on his next attempt?

It made more sense that Kaylee had been targeted because she was being too nosy about Amber's death, and neither her attack nor Amber's had anything to do with Ginger.

The captain's voice came over the speaker. "We appreciate everyone's cooperation and patience. We thought you'd like to know your fellow classmate is going to be fine. There doesn't appear to be any need for concern that today's meal will cause problems for anyone else. Detective Booker has given us permission to set sail once again. We will increase our speed as much as the sea conditions allow, so hopefully you will still arrive in time to catch the football game."

A cheer rose from the deck.

The instant the yacht docked on Orcas Island, Mary summoned Kaylee and Reese and the rest of the Petal Pushers to the flower shop.

DeeDee prodded them on toward the desk at the back of the store. "Did you find something in one of the pictures?"

They all crowded around the computer screen. Mary had six photos up and clicked on the one in the top corner. An image of a couple aboard the yacht filled the screen. Mary zoomed in on the buffet table behind them. "Did you see the time stamp on that picture?" she asked.

"Quarter to noon," Jessica said.

"Right." Mary pointed to the bittersweet on the table. "And the berries are still on the vine. See?"

Everyone nodded.

Mary selected the second photo. "Then there's this one, taken four minutes later." Once again she zoomed in on the table behind a new couple standing in front of it.

"The berries are gone!" DeeDee exclaimed.

"Bingo." Mary shrank the picture and grinned broadly. "So we know the berries were taken sometime during those four minutes. And these other four pictures are the only ones I found of that vicinity of the ship in that time period." She enlarged the first one.

In it, one of the ship's crew members appeared to be adding a plate to the table, while Wilma straightened nearby decorations.

"I just can't see Wilma poisoning Ginger," Jessica said. "Having someone get sick at a reunion event she planned wouldn't reflect well on her."

"Except revenge can be a compelling motive," Reese said.

"Did Ginger steal any of Wilma's boyfriends back in high school, DeeDee?"

"Wilma was too shy to have a boyfriend. Besides, I think she spent her entire senior year crushing on Arnold. And he was too geeky for Ginger to give him the time of day."

Mary enlarged the next picture on the computer screen. In it, Nina and Reggie were helping themselves to crab legs.

"Now Ginger did flirt with Reggie a lot in high school," DeeDee said.

"And still does," Kaylee added. "I could see Nina wanting to take her down a notch by slipping a few berries into her cocktail sauce. But she's supposedly been at a spa in Europe for a couple of months, so I don't see how she could be Ginger's stalker."

"You're assuming her stalker poisoned her," Mary said. "And maybe that's exactly what whoever did it wanted you to think. Doesn't mean it's true."

"Hmm. Good point," Kaylee said. She massaged her temples. Her head was seriously starting to hurt trying to keep track of all the possibilities.

The bell above the door jingled and Kaylee glanced toward the front of the store. Seeing no one, she assumed the person had realized the shop was closed and left again. She returned her attention to the computer screen.

The next photo depicted Dave spooning cocktail sauce on a plate laden with shrimp.

Reese whistled. "Do you think that's for Ginger?"

"Why would Dave poison her?" DeeDee asked. "Unless he wanted to be fired. I mean he's paid to protect her."

"Unless someone paid him better to torment her," Jessica speculated, in true conspiracy-theorist form.

"Or," DeeDee said, drawing the word out dramatically, "maybe he's been behind all the stalker notes and stuff to keep

Ginger on edge, so she'd be convinced she desperately needs him on the job."

Reese snorted. "That'd be ingenious."

"Think about it," Jessica said excitedly. "His and Ginger's fingerprints were the only ones on the note Ginger found in her beach bag. Remember?"

"Except if he got caught, he'd never work in the industry again," Mary said. "In security, your reputation is everything."

Mary enlarged the final picture and an image of Phil and Cheryl appeared.

"Phil seems to be taking something off the table behind that plate," DeeDee observed. "Too bad we can't see who Cheryl is talking to."

Sure enough, Cheryl's attention was directed to someone offscreen.

Kaylee squinted at the silver water pitcher standing on the table behind her. "Can you zoom in on the pitcher?" Kaylee asked Mary. "Maybe we can see a reflection on it."

A grainy image of Cheryl's hand hovering over someone else's materialized.

"She's handing off the berries to someone else!" DeeDee exclaimed.

"Maybe." Kaylee squinted at the image. "I can't tell if she's actually passing the person something."

"I think that's a guy's hand," Reese said. "The fingers are too thick for a woman's. But look. He's wearing a pinky ring. That should narrow the field."

"Why would Cheryl want to poison Ginger?" Mary asked.

Kaylee tapped her lip, not sure she should voice her thoughts. They felt a lot like Jessica's conspiracy theories, but then again . . .

"What are you thinking?" Jessica asked.

"This could be crazy, but if Phil and Cheryl killed Amber,

then overheard all the speculation about Ginger's stalker, they could have decided to capitalize on it by staging an incident that implicates him. It seems crazy to risk doing anything more that could get them investigated, but that's kind of what makes it so perfect. There's no reason to suspect them of wanting to hurt Ginger, so it shifts attention away from them as suspects to her stalker. And since people are assuming Amber's killer and Ginger's stalker are the same person, it also clears them for the murder."

"It sounds plausible anyway," DeeDee said.

"What sounds plausible?" a male voice said from behind them.

With a gasp, Kaylee spun around. Ewan. How had he gotten in without them noticing?

Or had that been what she'd heard—she glanced at the computer screen—three pictures ago?

"The game over already?" Reese asked casually.

"I've never been into football." Ewan raked his hair back from his face, and an uncomfortably familiar pinky ring glinted in the afternoon sun slanting through the windows.

How much had Ewan overheard?

Had they let slip to a murderer that they were trying to expose him?

16

"How can I help you?" Kaylee asked, crossing the store to put herself between the images on the computer screen and Ewan's prying eyes.

"I was wondering if you'd care to join me for dinner tonight before the closing ceremonies. There's a quaint seafood restaurant in Eastsound I like to visit when I'm here."

"Oh. Uh. That sounds lovely," Kaylee stuttered, "but I already have dinner plans this evening." She felt bad lying to him, but there was no way she was going to let herself be alone with the man after seeing his ring.

Reese stepped up beside her. "I'm sorry. She's giving me moral support for a family dinner."

Ewan grinned. "I understand. I wouldn't expect such a lovely woman to have her evening open on such late notice anyway, but I thought it was worth a shot." He glanced around and snatched up the closest thing at hand—a box of DeeDee's soaps. "I know you're not open today, but can I still get a couple of these? I'm not sure I'll have time to swing by again and purchase them before I leave."

"Good choice," DeeDee said, joining them at the counter. "Those are made with goat milk and scented with lavender grown right here on the island." She reached for one from his hand as if to point out something else about it and tilted her head. "What an interesting pinky ring."

Jessica muffled a gasp. Kaylee wasn't sure if it was because she hadn't seen the ring before or because of DeeDee's audacity.

"I don't think I've ever seen anything like it," DeeDee went on.

"No?" Ewan held out his hand for her to examine. "Your year didn't sell class rings?"

"Is that what this is? A class ring?"

"Yeah. I usually wear my college one, but I figured I'd put this one on for the reunion. A bunch of us guys did. I was surprised that some of them could even find theirs."

The tightness in Kaylee's chest eased a fraction at that news. *Except that more guys wearing them means more potential suspects to scrutinize.*

Ewan paid for the soaps and then leaned over the counter toward Kaylee and lowered his voice. "I know I pretended I didn't hear your conversation earlier, but I couldn't help but overhear you suspect Phil and Cheryl of hurting Ginger."

Kaylee's heart thumped.

"May I ask why you suspect them?"

"I'm sorry. I shouldn't have said that. It's nothing more than idle theorizing."

"But I think you could be on to something."

"Why?"

"Remember when we were all hiking at Cascade Lake, before Ginger found the note?"

Kaylee narrowed her eyes. "How'd you know about the note?"

He appeared momentarily taken aback by the question. "I heard people talking about it. They turned it in to the sheriff, right?"

"Hmm." She glanced back at her friends. It wasn't hard to imagine someone letting the information slip out.

"Anyway," Ewan continued, "Phil returned to the beach before the rest of us."

"Giving him opportunity," Kaylee finished for him.

"Bingo. Rumors about Ginger's stalker made the rounds on the bus ride to the park, thanks to the flowers someone saw her bodyguard refuse to accept."

"So you think the note was a plant?" Kaylee asked.

"You've gotta wonder. I mean, if Phil attacked Amber, his guilty conscience had to have been getting to him. And like you said, it could have gotten him thinking of ways to direct the investigators' attention away from him and his classmates."

Or Ewan could be trying to do exactly that by convincing her to dismiss her suspicions of him. She manufactured a smile and escorted him to the front of the store. "I appreciate your thoughts on this. I hope you have a nice day, and I'm sorry again about dinner."

He tipped her a charming smile. "Maybe I'll drop by the next time I'm on the island." He headed off.

Kaylee was about to lock the door behind Ewan when Wilma came scurrying up the sidewalk.

"Is Reese here?" she asked. "We saw his truck, and Arnold thought they could go for a walk while I see DeeDee."

"Yeah, he's here." Kaylee held the door open for her. "So is DeeDee."

"Oh good."

Reese slipped past them and joined Arnold on the sidewalk.

"I'll come find you when I'm done," Wilma called after him.

"Sure. Take your time. We can grab a bite to eat after," Arnold said. He and Reese strolled away.

DeeDee grinned at Wilma. "You and Arnold seem to be hitting it off."

Wilma's "yeah" was half-smile, half-wince.

"Uh-oh." DeeDee tugged her deeper into the store. "What's wrong?"

Wilma glanced skeptically at Kaylee, Jessica, and Mary.

"We're all friends now," DeeDee reassured her. "Whatever you say won't get past our lips."

"It might be nothing. I'm sure it's nothing. I need to borrow a computer for a few minutes and then I'll know for sure."

"Use this one." Kaylee led her to it and cleared the screen, then gestured toward the consultation area. "We'll be over there if you need us."

"Any clue what's got her so antsy?" Jessica asked when Kaylee joined them.

DeeDee was squinting at Wilma across the room on the computer when her eyes suddenly widened, and she leaned forward. "Did Sheriff Maddox ever find Amber's camera?" she whispered.

"Not that he's told me. Why?"

"Wilma just put an SD card in your computer that might have come from a camera. But previously she said she didn't own one."

"Maybe one of the other alumni loaned her theirs so she could upload the photos for them," Kaylee suggested.

"Why would she need privacy to do that?" Jessica whispered. "And what does that have to do with Arnold?"

"Maybe she's worried one of the photos incriminates him," Mary suggested. "I was thinking that she'd had the opportunity to screen all the photos sent to her earlier, until we asked to see them."

"And it was soon after that that her laptop supposedly got stolen," Jessica chimed in. "Conveniently rendering any incriminating photos inaccessible."

"Except the alumni still had their originals," Mary added. "Something the supposed hacker might have been trying to remedy."

"Supposed?" DeeDee sounded equal parts shocked and indignant.

"She is a librarian," Jessica reminded her. "She'd be able to research how to do pretty much anything."

"Trust me," DeeDee said. "Wilma did not fake her own burglary. And she has zero hacking skills. There's got to be a logical explanation." DeeDee strode over to Wilma and the rest of them followed.

The photos Amber had taken at the flower shop filled the screen.

"How did you get Amber's SD card?" Kaylee demanded.

Wilma's voice was shaky. "This isn't what it looks like."

"That's good, because it looks like you're in possession of property stolen from a dead woman," Kaylee said firmly.

Wilma gulped, and her eyes grew watery. "That can't be it. He's a good man."

"Who's a good man?" DeeDee asked, though Kaylee suspected her friends were all thinking the same thing she was.

"Arnold." Wilma cupped her hand over her mouth and shook her head at the images on the screen. "We were at the football game and I was getting chilly. So he put his jacket around me. It was so sweet." She inhaled, as if recalling how it had felt to be surrounded by his warmth and lingering scent. "I shoved my hands into the pockets to warm up and that's where I found the SD card. I was so scared what it could mean if it was Amber's. I had to be sure before I confronted him." Tears slipped from the corners of her eyes. "He couldn't have killed her. Why would he? He's not even in any of the pictures. Well, hardly any."

"We need to call Eddie," Mary said.

"Hold on a minute." Kaylee studied Wilma, trying to decide if she believed her story. It made sense, because, although her unrequited love for Arnold gave her motive to resent Amber, if she'd been behind the attack and had taken her camera, she would have destroyed the evidence by now. She certainly wouldn't have brought it out right under their noses.

Finally she said, "I agree we need to call the sheriff, but I'd like to download copies of the images first and go through them. See if we can spot anything that might point to who attacked her."

"Yes. Yes," Wilma managed to say through the tears running down her cheeks. "Because it wasn't Arnold. You have to prove it wasn't Arnold. I can't lose him. Not now that he's finally noticed me."

They all gathered around the computer screen and scrolled through the images one by one.

"Stop," DeeDee said. "Isn't that near where you spotted Amber in the hogweed at the park the first day?"

"You're right." Kaylee zoomed in on the couple Amber appeared to be photographing through the trees.

"It's Cheryl," Wilma said. "I can tell by the sweater. But I don't think that's Phil with her, unless he's standing on a rock. This guy must be almost a foot taller than her."

Ewan is a tall guy. Kaylee kept the thought to herself for now. He'd outright said the day Amber's body was found that a cheating spouse might kill to get rid of incriminating pictures. Had he thought the fact he wasn't married would exclude him from suspicion?

Kaylee zoomed in, but the picture was too pixelated to make out the guy's profile through the trees. She moved on.

"Whoa!" Jessica exclaimed as a photo of Dave and Ginger kissing appeared on the screen. "No wonder Ginger was paranoid about Amber posting pictures of her."

Mary snorted. "They're adults. If they want to date, why shouldn't they? And why should she care about anyone finding out?"

"Because according to the tabloids, she's in a romantic relationship with her soap opera costar," Jessica said.

"That could just be a publicity stunt," DeeDee said.

"Sure," Jessica agreed. "But her show's producers are probably milking it for all it's worth, and they wouldn't appreciate a photo like this coming out. On the other hand, it might mean more publicity, though it wouldn't do much for Ginger's reputation."

They continued to scroll through the pictures. There was one of Cheryl chatting with Reggie, several of Ewan chatting with various female alumni, one of Ginger dancing with Reggie, followed by one of Nina glaring at the soap opera star. The only pictures of Arnold were one of him sitting with the group in the burger joint their first night and his staged portrait in the flower shop.

"See," Wilma said. "There's nothing in there that Arnold needed to be concerned over. He couldn't have been the guy with Cheryl in the bushes. He's only an inch taller than me."

"Did you notice what else wasn't in there?" Mary asked.

Kaylee nodded. "Not a single incriminating photo of Phil. In every one he's in, he's wincing in pain or hobbling or sitting alone—nothing to suggest he's living it up on an undeserved disability pension."

"So we're back to the cheating spouse theory?" DeeDee asked.

"Or Ginger," Jessica interjected. "I don't know the woman personally, but I get the sense that a lot of Hollywood types have a pretty strong sense of entitlement."

"Do you think she poisoned herself?" DeeDee asked.

Jessica frowned. "No, I don't think she could do it to herself. Are you sure she wasn't acting? Or maybe her poisoning isn't connected to Amber's death. Her stalker might've actually caught up to her."

"We'd better call Eddie now." Kaylee ejected the SD card from her computer. "After tonight's Hall of Fame Induction Ceremony, half the alumni will be heading back to the mainland."

Someone knocked on the shop door.

"It's Reese and Arnold," Mary said.

Wilma swiped at her damp eyes with her sleeve. "He can't see me like this."

DeeDee steered her toward the restroom.

"Don't say anything to him until I get back," she said. "I want him to know I believe in him no matter what."

Mary unlocked the front door.

Reese stepped in and glanced around. "Did Wilma leave?"

"We don't have a lot of time left to get dinner before tonight's events," Arnold added.

"I'm afraid dinner will need to wait a little longer," Kaylee said. "We need to talk to you about something Wilma found in your coat pocket."

"In my coat pocket?" He pushed his hands into his pockets and turned them inside out. "There's nothing in them."

Wilma joined them, her complexion white. "It was the SD card from Amber's camera," she said so quietly Kaylee wasn't sure if Arnold had heard.

"What? How?"

"Did she give it to you before she left the restaurant?" Kaylee asked.

"No!"

"You're sure?"

"I'd know if she gave me her SD card," Arnold said impatiently.

"I know you didn't attack her, Arnold," Wilma said, her voice cracking. "I know you would never do that. Someone must have planted it in your pocket to frame you."

"Yeah. Amber," Reese said.

"What?" Kaylee spun to face him, stunned by the theory.

"Remember her sleight-of-hand tricks at the table?" Reese asked. "She told us no move was by accident. And she'd fiddled with her camera just before she started. Maybe she sensed the wrong person was on to why she was really taking photos and slipped the SD card into Arnold's pocket for safekeeping."

"He could be right," Arnold said. "She pickpocketed me as a joke all the time."

"But why not tell him what she'd done?" Kaylee asked.

Reese grimaced. "Maybe she never got the chance."

17

The sheriff seemed to take both Wilma and Arnold at their word and thanked them for passing along the SD card—although he did make a point of confirming Arnold didn't plan to leave the island until the following day.

Kaylee wondered if he planned to ask his computer expert to see if he could recover any photos that were deleted from the card—photos that, unlike the ones they'd seen, might incriminate one of them.

The Petals, Reese, Arnold, and Wilma followed him out of the flower shop, debating where to eat before the Hall of Fame Induction Ceremonies at the high school that evening.

"Guys." Jessica pointed across the street. "Ginger's back."

"Thank goodness," Wilma said. "I was worried she'd miss tonight's ceremony. She's one of the inductees from our graduating class, along with Reggie for some breakthrough technology he's developed. He plans to do the big reveal about it tonight."

"Really?" DeeDee said. "I'd have thought he'd want to do something that newsworthy someplace with plenty of reporters."

Wilma rolled her eyes. "Knowing Reggie, he's probably invited a slew of mainland reporters to cover the event. And the paparazzi have swarmed here in droves since news leaked of Ginger's 'brush with death.'"

A slender, blond guy hurried up to Ginger with a pen and small leather-bound book. "Miss Andrews, I've admired your work for so long. May I have your autograph?" he gushed.

With a camera-worthy smile, she thumbed through to a clean page, where she probably wrote a personal message along with her name, judging by how long it took her to write it.

As she handed it back, he thanked her profusely and requested permission to take a picture with her. After she nodded her approval, he circled his arm around her shoulder and held his cell phone camera at arm's length.

Mary grabbed Kaylee's arm. "That's the guy."

"What guy?"

"The guy who ordered the flowers for Ginger—the ones you said were sent by her stalker."

"Seriously?" Kaylee's gaze darted from the guy to Mary to Ginger's bodyguard. "I've got to tell Dave."

"I'll call the sheriff."

Kaylee hurried across the street.

"Did you like the flowers I sent you?" the guy asked as Kaylee reached them.

Gasping, Ginger took a huge step away from him.

Dave grabbed the man and slammed him up against the nearest wall.

"What are you doing?" the guy demanded.

Dave, in one deft move, spun the guy to face the wall, kicked apart his legs, and patted him for weapons. "Miss Andrews doesn't appreciate stalkers making veiled threats about her safety while out on the beach."

"What are you talking about? I never threatened her. I love her. I'm her biggest fan."

Dave pressed the man's cheek against the rough brick. "You've got a funny way of showing it."

"All I did was send flowers," he whined.

"What about the note in her beach bag? Huh?" Dave demanded.

"You've got the wrong guy. I didn't send a note. I swear!"

"No? And I suppose you didn't poison her shrimp cocktail either?"

"No!"

"Dave," Kaylee said softly. "I don't think he was on the boat with us."

"He could have hired someone to do his dirty work. Is that what you did?" Dave demanded. "Hire someone?"

The sheriff's car screeched around the corner and stopped beside them, sirens blaring. "What's going on?" Sheriff Maddox demanded as he climbed out of the vehicle.

Dave relayed his suspicions over the other man's protestations.

Eddie handcuffed the guy. "We'll sort this out at the station." He jutted his chin toward Dave. "You two can follow me in your car."

"But—" Ginger stared at him, the picture of a panicked actress who'd forgotten her line.

Wilma hurried across the street to join them. "Ginger can't go. She's being inducted into the high school's Hall of Fame tonight. She can't miss the ceremony."

"When is it?" Eddie asked.

"Seven."

He glanced at his watch. "She'll have plenty of time to get there." He shoved the guy into the back seat of his cruiser. "Let's go."

Kaylee stared after their cars as they drove off.

"Why don't you seem happy?" Reese asked. "We've identified Ginger's stalker and maybe even Amber's killer."

"He said he didn't write the note that was in her beach bag," Kaylee said. She couldn't ignore that if it was true, that information fit with their theory about Phil.

"Prisons are full of people who swear they didn't do whatever they're in for," Mary argued.

"But what if he was telling the truth? The card with the flowers he sent was signed M, but the note Ginger found in her beach bag wasn't signed. Neither was the one on the ship."

"Because whoever was trying to frame him didn't know

he signed his initial," Jessica speculated, watching the sheriff's departing cruiser. "And the sheriff is going to be wasting his time following a rabbit trail that'll get him nowhere."

"Exactly. And time is something we have very little of if we hope to nail Amber's murderer before half our suspects leave the island." Kaylee tugged Bear's lead and headed toward her car. "You guys go get your supper. I need to drop Bear off at home, then pay the hotel another visit. I'll catch up with you at the high school tonight."

Reese looped his arm through hers and tugged her toward his truck. "I'll drive you." He held open the passenger door for her and Bear. "This guy has already tried to take you out at least once," he said as he climbed into the driver's seat. "What are you thinking?"

"If that guy really didn't write the note Ginger found in her beach bag, then maybe Phil and Cheryl wrote it like Ewan suggested."

Reese drove toward the hotel after they took Bear to Wildflower Cottage. "The police already searched their room and didn't turn up anything. Where else do you plan to look?"

"Only in their room. Think about it. The police weren't thinking about the possibility Phil wrote a threatening note to Ginger when they conducted their search. So they wouldn't have had any reason to scrutinize the hotel notepad in the room."

"Ah, you want to try the old pencil-shading trick."

Kaylee grinned. "You've been brushing up on your mystery novels."

"How do you plan to get into their room?"

"I'm hoping I can sweet-talk the manager into having the housekeeper check the room's supplies and, in particular, supply them with a fresh notepad."

"While relieving them of their current one?"

"Exactly."

Reese parked near the door and surveyed their surroundings,

then peered through the lobby window before holding the door open for her.

"You're jumpy," she observed.

"No, I'm just not taking any chances."

Thankfully, the manager was at the desk. Kaylee presented her request.

"I can do you one better," Brian said and magnetized a fresh key card. "Go let yourselves in. Room 206. The couple checked out a half hour ago."

"Checked out?" Kaylee's pulse jumped.

"Yes. They said they'd decided to take a ferry back to the mainland tonight. Their room won't be cleaned until tomorrow morning."

"Perfect. Thank you."

She and Reese took the stairs two at a time. "We've got to hurry. They could be getting on the next ferry."

"Hopefully, they wouldn't want to draw any extra attention by skipping the final reunion event," Reese said, passing her a second before she reached the door to the second floor. He stepped ahead of her and peeked through the door, then invited her to precede him into the hallway.

They found the room and let themselves in. Her hopes flagged. "I don't see the notepad. Check the trash cans." Kaylee yanked open the shallow drawer in the middle of the desk. "Found it!"

"Wait." Reese snatched a tissue from a nearby box and handed them to her. "We don't want to add any fingerprints to it."

"Good thinking." Kaylee used the tissue to pull the notepad from the drawer and set it on the desktop. Then she helped herself to a pencil from the drawer and, holding the pencil parallel to the desk, began lightly shading over any possible indentations.

No telltale words appeared.

She sighed. "Nothing. Housekeeping must have already

replaced their pad since Friday."

"Or they didn't write the note," Reese countered in a reasonable voice. He sat on the bed and opened the night table drawer. "Here's another one." He grabbed a fresh tissue and brought the pad to the desk.

Kaylee repeated the shading routine.

Dozens of doodle lines appeared.

"Try a page deeper in the pad," Reese suggested.

"Good thinking." Kaylee flipped through, squinting at each page, planning to shade every one if necessary. She opted to start with the bottom page. Excitement welled in her chest. "I can see words!"

Reese read them as they materialized. "'See what walking a quiet beach alone at night gets a girl?'"

"It's the note Ginger found in her bag. We have to call the sheriff. Tell him to get down to the ferry and pick up Phil and Cheryl before they leave the island."

Reese pulled out his phone and scrolled through his contact list, then tapped the screen and brought the phone to his ear. "Unfortunately, I doubt the note is sufficient evidence to hold them."

"It should be enough to warrant scraping their fingernails and testing their clothes for traces of bittersweet." Kaylee glanced around. "And to give this room another thorough going over before housekeeping gets in here."

Reese talked to the sheriff briefly and then returned his phone to his pocket. "Eddie wants us to wait for him here."

"But—"

Reese raised his hand to stop her protest. "He's sending a deputy to the ferry to collect them if they're there."

Kaylee paced. "Is he coming right away?"

Reese chuckled. "He is."

"It seems too easy."

"Excuse me?"

"They didn't leave any fingerprints in Amber's room or on her phone, but they leave behind a notepad that points to them?"

"Criminals make mistakes."

Kaylee frowned. "Or Ewan set them up."

Reese's head jerked as if he were stunned by the suggestion. "How do you figure?"

"He was the one who theorized that they wrote the note. He had to figure we'd go looking or tell the sheriff. He knows his way around pain meds, and he'd have to know poisons too, since he's a vet."

"How would he have accessed their room?"

Kaylee shrugged. "He has enough nerve to walk in on the housekeeper and say he needed to grab something off the night table. Maybe he used that as a cover to plant the notepad."

"Interesting theory, but everyone knew the police searched Phil and Cheryl's room last night. Don't you think he would have assumed they'd confiscated the notepads for further scrutiny?"

"Unless he planted it before last night, and then when the police didn't discover the clue, he figured he needed to 'help' them."

"Why would he go to so much trouble to frame Phil and Cheryl when he isn't a person of interest?"

Kaylee stared at herself in the mirror above the bureau and folded her arms over her chest, not liking how suspicious she'd become of anyone and everyone. "Fine. Ewan might be innocent."

"The evidence, as circumstantial as it is, points much more overwhelmingly toward Phil and Cheryl," Reese said.

"Mr. Fletcher did say Cheryl was his brightest student. She'd probably be able to recognize the bittersweet berries and know what their effect would be."

"And the mushrooms in your water bottle," Reese said grimly.

Kaylee shuddered. She had managed to shut out thoughts

of her own poisoning and its possible connection to everything else. Or maybe that was an aftereffect of the mushrooms too.

There was a knock on the door, and Reese went to answer it. "And if Reggie managed to undo DeeDee's computer hack, then it seems to me that Phil, who did the same kind of work, would've been capable of gaining control of it in the first place," Reese said to Kaylee as he opened the door. "Hi, sheriff."

"Except the couple didn't have a computer on the island," the sheriff said.

"They did if they stole Wilma's laptop," Kaylee reminded him. "Only"—she frowned—"they were here that night. I saw them. They didn't go to the mini-golf tournament because of Cheryl's rash."

"They did go into town that evening to pick up a pizza for dinner," the sheriff said. "Whereas Ginger's flower sender, Martin Munroe, or 'M' as he signed his notes, alibied out for the beach day, this morning's cruise, and the night of the robbery as well as the night of your poisoning."

"Kind of sounds a little too convenient, don't you think?" Reese said. "Even if I hadn't been at half those events, I probably couldn't have given you an ironclad alibi for every single one. It sounds like he made a point of ensuring he'd have one."

Eddie nodded. "That thought had crossed my mind, but it turns out he's been playing in a three-day golf tournament in Eastsound. The other members of his group and the golf club's staff have all vouched for him." Eddie studied the notepad and then slipped it into an evidence bag. "You should have left finding this to me, Kaylee. You could have put yourself back in their crosshairs by coming here."

"You had an interrogation, and time was of the essence," Kaylee said impatiently. "Can we go now? We told Arnold and Wilma we'd meet up with them at the high school."

"Yeah, I'm heading there myself to see if Phil and Cheryl show up. I've got a deputy watching the ferry line."

"The crazy thing is that, after seeing Amber's photos, I doubt her investigation would have cost Phil his disability payments," Reese observed. "And killing her wouldn't help if the insurance company sends out another investigator to finish her job."

"Assuming that was their motive," Kaylee said.

"What else would it be?"

Kaylee sighed. "I'm not sure. But my gut tells me it has something to do with the guy Cheryl was talking to in the bushes. And I'm thinking he wears a class ring."

"Leave the investigating to me and my deputies," the sheriff ordered. "You've already ticked off the wrong person. What if they try again? You might not be so lucky next time."

18

By the time Kaylee and Reese arrived at the high school for the Hall of Fame ceremony, the emcee was already welcoming everyone. Wilma spotted them and waved them over to a pair of seats they'd saved next to Phil and Cheryl.

"They're here," Kaylee whispered to Reese. She glanced to the back of the auditorium where Sheriff Maddox had walked in behind Jocko McGee. Kaylee waited until Jocko wasn't paying attention to her, then subtly pointed out the pair to the sheriff.

Eddie nodded and, crossing his arms over his chest, planted himself in front of the rear entrance.

"I guess he doesn't want to disturb the ceremonies by pulling them out," Reese murmured. He took the empty one next to Phil and Kaylee sat beside Wilma.

The auditorium was packed with townsfolk and graduates from the past five or six decades. "Wow," Kaylee remarked. "This thing is a really big deal."

"You bet," Wilma replied, giving her a small smile.

They acknowledged select former graduates in chronological order by graduating class. Among the recipients was everyone from a Nobel Prize winner to an astronaut. When they reached Arnold and Wilma's class year, Ginger was the first to be called up for her success in television.

Wilma leaned over and whispered, "Ginger and Dave joined us for dinner, and we learned something interesting. Turns out that platter of shrimp Dave was carrying in the photo was meant for Ginger, only he turned too suddenly from the buffet table and bumped into Cheryl, who spilled her drink down the front of his shirt."

"Really?"

"He said he put the plate down for a moment to try to clean up his shirt. It's the only time he can think of when he'd been distracted enough that someone had the opportunity to slip the poison into the cocktail sauce."

Kaylee's stomach knotted as she glanced down the row at Cheryl and Phil, or more precisely at their hands folded in their laps. Cheryl wore nail polish so it was impossible to tell if she had any telltale berry juice stains under her nails. Phil wore only a wedding band. But since he didn't attend Turtle Cove High, she wouldn't have expected him to have a class ring.

Ginger accepted her certificate to thunderous applause and a blinding number of camera flashes. Her hair, clothing, and makeup were meticulous. No one would have ever guessed she'd spent half the afternoon in the hospital.

Three more former classmates were recognized, then to the sound of a drumroll, the emcee said, "And last but not least for this class, we'd like to recognize our former star quarterback and prom king who went on to take the technology world by storm. His business has become a Fortune 500 company, and tonight as he accepts his induction into our Hall of Fame, he is going to treat us to the first announcement of his newest breakthrough. Please join me in welcoming Reggie Blake." The emcee led the clapping which went on for a good minute after Reggie reached the podium and said "thank you" several times.

"Popular guy," Reese said to Kaylee.

Wilma snorted, clearly not impressed by the man, whereas Arnold stared at him as if he'd hung the moon.

Reggie went on for several minutes about the rapid advancements in technology since he'd graduated high school and the new challenges the industry faced, complete with images on the big screen above the stage. "For years, the holy grail for electrical engineers has been to develop a superconductor, something with negligible resistance that would make the resulting power loss of our current old-fashioned electrical conductors a distant memory."

As the audience murmured around them, Phil gasped. "No way!" he hissed to Cheryl. "How'd they do it? Our company masterminded that technology. We are mere months away from unveiling our new conductor. There's no way his company could have simultaneously . . ." His hands fisted. "He must've gotten to one of our researchers. The company was counting on the innovation. This could bankrupt it."

Cheryl patted his leg. "He probably just caught wind that we were on the verge of unveiling something and decided to beat us to the gate with the announcement and worry about being able to deliver later. He's done that before, remember? You know how he likes to talk big. Besides, now that you're retired, it's not as if you have to worry about what happens to the company."

"Okay," the emcee said as Reggie returned to his seat. "We're going to take a short intermission before we continue with the remaining presentations. Don't forget to take a few moments to wander down the newly created Hall of Fame to my left outside the auditorium. See you here again in fifteen minutes."

Wilma and Arnold wandered off to go through the Hall of Fame.

Kaylee rose to stretch and discreetly survey the alumni sitting nearby. Reggie sat a little way down their row, beyond where Wilma and Arnold and another couple had been. He made no move to get up, so Kaylee sidled his way and stuck out her hand. "Congratulations."

A smile worthy of a toothpaste commercial appeared on his face as he gripped her hand a little too firmly. "This seemed like a great venue to make the big announcement. Give the old alma mater some free national publicity."

And stick it to your former partner.

He hefted his foot across his knee, and the overhead lights glinted off the school ring on his pinky.

Could he have been the one Cheryl appeared to be handing something to in the photograph? Given the rivalry between their companies, Kaylee had gotten the impression from Phil that they avoided each other. Then again, Cheryl had wandered over and chatted with Reggie after Phil headed back to the beach the day of their hike.

Reggie chattered on about his technological breakthrough. Kaylee nodded whenever he paused as her mind raced to evaluate him as a suspect. He seemed to enjoy Ginger's flirtations, making it difficult to imagine he'd willingly taint her food. Then again, plenty of ruthless businessmen were willing to do whatever it took to further their interests.

But what were his interests?

She dropped her gaze, realizing she'd missed most of what he'd said. She found herself examining the shoe he'd propped on his other knee. Something sparkled. Were those bits of glass caught in the treads?

Her pulse quickened as she remembered the glass on the rock next to Amber's body.

It had to be a coincidence. She probably had shards in her shoes herself, thanks to the glass she'd shattered at the dinner Saturday night.

After all, what possible motive could Reggie have for killing Amber?

The PI wasn't investigating him—unless he'd been the one talking to Cheryl in that grainy picture in the woods. Although it was hardly proof of anything going on between them . . . if it was even him.

Sure, people might question the rendezvous, given their respective companies' rivalry, but this was a reunion. He could have easily explained it away as catching up with an old classmate.

Then again, a grainy photo like that might be all it took to send his insecure wife off the deep end. Surely the photo of him and Ginger dancing would be worse. Still, he was a smooth talker. Maybe he'd made Nina see reason.

Or maybe he couldn't. She'd already blown up on Amber in the restroom at the restaurant. Maybe she'd had a second go at her on the beach, which left it up to her husband to cover up a crime of passion and make it look like a robbery.

Except that didn't explain the glass shards and wet footprints on Amber's carpet. And poison wasn't how a crime of passion would be committed.

"Is something wrong with my shoe?" Reggie asked, making Kaylee jump.

She forced a smile. "No, sorry. You caught me daydreaming." She tamped down the impulse to point out the glass. Alerting him to it could go wrong in too many ways if he was guilty.

His wife, sitting on the other side of him, squeezed his shoulder. "I'm going to the little girls' room."

"I should too. Before the intermission ends," Kaylee agreed. Reggie's scowl might have been the product of her overactive imagination, but either way, she was relieved to put some distance between them.

Kaylee and Nina filled in the end of the line of women waiting to use the facilities and Kaylee took the opportunity to text Reese about the glass shards.

His annoyingly reasonable text back—he could have picked those up anywhere in the last three days—made her wonder why she felt so resistant to believing Phil and Cheryl were behind all the attacks. Or at least Phil.

With only Nina and herself left waiting for free stalls, Kaylee asked, "Have you been able to enjoy a moonlit walk along the beach since you arrived?"

"I wanted to the first night, but it was raining," she said without a second's hesitation or flinch of guilt. "Not my idea of walking weather."

"Right. I just remember you and your husband left the dance kind of early, and I hoped you'd been able to do something nice."

"We went back to our hotel room and I had a nice long hot shower, while Reg put a bottle of wine on ice."

He would have had to leave the room to fill the ice bucket. And if he'd spied Amber on the beach, Nina's nice long shower would have left him enough time to jog out there and back.

A stall opened up and Nina let herself in. Kaylee slipped out, intending to check in with the sheriff.

She ran smack into Reggie, who stood right outside the door. "Is Nina all right?" he asked mildly.

"Nina? Oh sure." Kaylee took a deep breath. She sounded guilty. "The line was crazy, so I gave up waiting. She should be out in a minute."

He scrutinized her face as if trying to read what she wasn't saying, or maybe that was her wild imagination again.

"Excuse me," she said. "Reese will be wondering what's keeping me."

Kaylee scanned the back of the auditorium for Eddie as the emcee urged everyone to resume their seats. Unable to spot the sheriff, Kaylee edged back to her seat. "Where'd Eddie get to?" she whispered to Reese.

"He texted me, said he had an urgent call he had to respond to. He'll be back before the ceremonies are scheduled to end."

Kaylee lowered her voice. "But will Phil and Cheryl stay that long?"

"All right, let's get back to it," the emcee said.

Phil rose and stepped into the aisle to let Nina and Reggie

scoot past him on their way back to their seats. "Congratulations on your success."

Reggie clapped Phil's shoulder and shook his hand. "Thanks, man. Ultimately, the whole world wins, right?"

It's a wonder the man has the strength to carry around that big an ego day and night.

"If it works," was Phil's response.

Reggie chuckled. "It will. I only work with the best people." He nodded to Cheryl, then slipped past her chair behind his wife.

After they'd edged past Reese and Kaylee as well, Cheryl scolded Phil. "You sounded as if you'd swallowed a mouthful of sour grapes."

"He got to someone in our company and bribed them for our research. I know it," Phil replied shortly.

"Or maybe his researchers were as capable as ours—but I'd still bet our technology is better than his."

The ceremonies resumed with no sign of Wilma and Arnold rejoining Kaylee and Reese. Kaylee leaned over to him. "I think Wilma finally got her wish and your friend has noticed how much she adores him."

"Yeah, I guess he took our little talk to heart."

Kaylee lifted her eyebrows. "You talked to him about Wilma?"

Reese grinned at her. "You don't have to sound so surprised. Men do talk about relationships on occasion."

Kaylee reined in the smile that tugged at her lips. "Glad to hear it." She realized the crowd had thinned considerably since the intermission. Maybe people were getting tired.

The emcee obviously noticed too, because he rushed through introducing the remaining inductees. As the final recipients returned to their seats, the emcee raised his hand to quiet the applause. "And now we'd like to honor one of Turtle Cove High's favorite teachers. Mr. Dwayne Fletcher taught science and environmental studies here for forty-three years and, for many years into his retirement, he continued to volunteer supervising several of the clubs and annual fund-raisers he'd helped found."

A slide show of old yearbook snapshots flashed on the big screen above the stage as the emcee continued. "We'll definitely miss him when he moves off the island this fall, but we'd like to thank our reunion coordinator and everyone who has helped make this special event happen before he leaves. And now, some of his students would like to say a few words about him."

The slide show continued as several former students went to the podium and shared favorite memories of their beloved teacher. Then Wilma joined the emcee on stage and invited Mr. Fletcher to come up and receive his plaque. She also presented him with a special arrangement Kaylee had made and a collage of then-and-now pictures of their graduating class, signed with heartwarming sentiments by everyone who'd made it to the reunion.

The audience sprang to their feet in a thunderous standing ovation that brought tears to the former teacher's eyes.

As the audience began to sit down, Cheryl and Phil gathered their sweaters and slipped toward the end of the row.

Kaylee leaned across Reese's lap and attempted to catch Cheryl's arm, but caught only air. She sprang to her feet and stage-whispered, "Wait! Are you leaving?"

Cheryl seemed to debate how to respond.

"Yes," Phil said for her. "We don't want to miss our ferry."

Cheryl scowled at him, then said to Kaylee, "It was nice to meet you." Only she said it through gritted teeth, as if the expected formality left a sour taste in her mouth.

A woman behind them swayed from side to side, clearly irritated she couldn't see the stage past Kaylee.

Kaylee dropped into her seat and squinted toward the back of the auditorium to see if the sheriff had returned and if he had noticed the pair getting up. Seeing Phil hobble out the end of the row, the reasons Kaylee doubted his guilt solidified in her mind. When she'd asked him about his pain management, he'd immediately admitted to wearing a pain patch. And he'd later told the sheriff he had a replacement in his suitcase—not something an intelligent person would have done if he'd used it to murder someone. But that made Kaylee all the more suspicious of Cheryl, who'd seemingly convinced the forgetful man he'd already applied his spare patch.

Maybe she'd acted alone. Kaylee recalled Amber's photo of Cheryl's rendezvous in the woods. A meeting so clandestine that she—Mr. Fletcher's star botany student—hadn't noticed the hogweed she'd tramped through.

Or was the mystery man her accomplice?

If Amber gave a bad report on her husband and Phil lost his insurance payments, Cheryl would suffer too, but was that her motive? How had she even known that Amber was a PI? Had Amber's dodgy answer when Cheryl had asked what she did for a living tipped Cheryl off? Or had something, or someone, else?

Phil started toward the rear of the auditorium, but Cheryl steered him toward the front.

Hoping to escape the sheriff's notice?

"We can't let them leave," Kaylee said to Reese. "I don't think Eddie is back yet."

"He is." Reese showed her the screen of his phone. "I texted him."

"Text him again and tell him they're going out the front of the auditorium. I'll try to stall them until he gets there."

Kaylee reached the aisle as everyone else poured out of their seats. She lost sight of the couple in the sea of heads. Reese caught up to her and pushed his way against the flow of people heading for the rear exits. She gratefully trailed him.

Wilma and Arnold intercepted them. "We thought we'd head

to the Pacific Street Diner for one last cheeseburger. You guys in?"

"Maybe later," Reese said, continuing to inch forward. "There's someone we need to catch up with before they leave." He pointed to a door off the front of the auditorium straight ahead. "Where does that lead?"

"The second wing," Wilma said, "but the lights won't be on over there."

"There's no exit to the parking lot?"

"There's one to the side parking lot."

"And the door on the other side" — Arnold pointed to the far side of the stage — "takes you to the back lot between the first and second wings."

Kaylee hopped onto the stage and scanned the crowd between them and the far corridor. "You take this door. I'll take the far one," she said to Reese and sprinted across the now empty stage to the other side of the auditorium.

As she descended the stairs on the other side, Reggie stepped into her path and grabbed her arm.

It was all Kaylee could do not to scream.

19

"Whoa, where's the fire?" Reggie asked.

Heart racing, Kaylee glanced up at the man looming over her. Her suspicions about him cascaded through her thoughts once more, but as his wife stepped up beside him, Kaylee shook away the silly notion. He'd be an idiot to confront her in a room full of people. And he clearly wasn't an idiot. And she had more important things to think about—like Phil and Cheryl getting away. Kaylee forced out a chuckle and pulled her arm from his grasp. "Just trying to—"

"Nina, dear," Reggie interrupted. "Isn't that Elaine over there?" He pointed toward the back of the auditorium. "You wanted to say goodbye to her before we left, didn't you? Go on over. I'll catch up in a minute."

Nina hurried off as Kaylee edged past Reggie. She spotted Phil and Cheryl exiting the door at the end of the dimly lit corridor and glanced across the stage to see if Reese had come back in. There was no sign of him, but Wilma and Arnold hovered near the exit.

Reggie beamed at her. "We never got to finish our discussion about the superconductor. I—"

"Excuse me," she interrupted. "I have to run." She raised her voice and called, "Wilma, tell Reese they're this way!"

Kaylee hurried out the door after them. It opened into an empty stairwell. Not hearing any sound coming from the stairs, she pushed open the door on the opposite side.

The door opened into a parking lot as Arnold had said and, thanks to Phil's leg, he and Cheryl hadn't gotten far. She texted her location to the sheriff and pushed open the door. When the door clicked shut behind Kaylee, they both glanced over their shoulders at her.

Kaylee smiled. "Nice evening, isn't it?"

"Sweetheart," Cheryl said, touching Phil's arm. "I need to use the facilities before we go. Do you mind bringing the car around to the door?"

"Sure." He continued on as Cheryl spun back toward Kaylee.

Reese came out the door a second before Cheryl reached it.

"There you are," Kaylee said brightly, as if she'd been standing around waiting for him so they could leave.

"You ready to go?" he asked, clueing in to the subterfuge.

"Actually, I think—"

Cheryl disappeared through the door.

Kaylee lowered her voice. "She said she has to use the facilities before they go. Phil is going for the car." She pointed behind her. "That way. I'll follow Cheryl. You keep an eye on Phil. I texted Eddie already."

Reese held open the door for her. "Be careful," he whispered as she passed inside.

Reggie stood on the other side of the opposite door, peering through the narrow window. Their gazes met.

Kaylee's heart skipped a beat.

"If you're looking for a restroom," Cheryl called down to Kaylee from halfway up the stairs, "there's another one up here that won't have the lines."

"Great. Thanks for the tip." Kaylee glanced back at the window, but Reggie was gone. She scaled the stairs two at a time, grateful for the easy excuse to follow the woman.

The stairs opened to an unlit hallway. To their right was a windowed hallway that crossed over the driveway from the back parking lot between the school's two wings. Cheryl turned down the hallway.

Kaylee hesitated. "It's kind of dark up here." If not for the evening twilight seeping through the windows, she wouldn't be able to see at all.

"The restroom is only a couple of doors beyond the walkway," Cheryl said. "I'm sure we can find the light switch inside."

Kaylee's pulse edged higher as she followed the woman. The sound of the heavy corridor door squeaking open below made her jump. She glanced out the window and spotted a cruiser coming, hopefully to block Phil and Cheryl's car from being able to leave. Maybe she would wait in the hall for Cheryl and text the sheriff again to let him know they were upstairs. No telling what Cheryl would do if she spotted the deputies through the window on their way out.

Cheryl stopped outside a door. "Coming?"

Kaylee hurried toward her. The door said *Room 211*, not *Girls' Restroom*. Kaylee glanced at the next door. It also said *Room 211*. "Are you sure this is it?"

"Yes, this is the home ec room. There are two entrances and it has a restroom off the kitchen."

"They probably don't want people wandering through the classrooms," Kaylee pointed out.

Cheryl tried the doorknob. "It's not locked. They can't be too concerned." She reached inside and flipped on the light, then walked in. "It's this way."

Kaylee glanced down the empty hallway then followed her in.

Cheryl dropped her oversized purse on the kitchen counter. "This was always my favorite class."

Kaylee stopped. "Really? But there are no windows." The room was the size of three rooms combined. One area was a kitchen. One area had a dozen sewing machines set up. A third section had tables and chairs facing a whiteboard. "You don't get any daylight in here."

Cheryl rounded the counter, closing the distance between them. "But that's what makes it so perfect."

"How do you figure?" The hair on the back of her neck prickled a warning. Too late.

"No light gets out either."

Cheryl jabbed something hard into Kaylee's side and an excruciating jolt of electricity seized her limbs.

Kaylee cried out, but she wasn't sure the sound made it past her lips as she collapsed to the floor. Then the lights faded.

I can't breathe.

She jolted back to consciousness and tore at the pillow pressed against her face. Unable to move it, she clawed at the person holding it and kicked wildly.

Then suddenly the weight pressing against her face lifted.

Kaylee rolled onto her side and scrambled away. Her head felt as if it was caught in a vice and when she attempted to rise, she toppled sideways, too dizzy to keep her balance.

"Are you crazy? What do you think you're doing?" a male voice barked.

A familiar male voice. Kaylee blinked, straining to bring the scene into focus.

"She knows," Cheryl hissed.

"And you think murdering her up here with your bare hands while your husband chats with the sheriff in the parking lot is going to keep you from getting caught?"

Reggie. Kaylee gulped. How had he found them?

"Are you going to take care of this or what?" Cheryl spat back.

Reggie was Cheryl's accomplice? Still too woozy to stand, and not liking the odds, Kaylee scooted toward the door.

Reggie snapped on a pair of latex gloves. "Don't I always take care of your messes? You need to learn not to overreact. It's what got you into this in the first place."

"How was I supposed to know that woman was only a PI for the insurance company?"

"Maybe because that's what your friend in the president's office told you?" Reggie sounded as if he was scarcely holding on to his patience.

"Sure, but if the president was on to me—"

"Like you assumed," Reggie filled in.

"Then he would have wanted everyone to think she was just doing her due diligence for the insurance company, wouldn't he?"

Kaylee's head spun, trying to make sense of what they were saying. What had Cheryl done that she feared her boss was "on to" her?

Phil's earlier declaration about Reggie getting to one of the company's researchers hit Kaylee's memory and she muffled a gasp.

Cheryl was the spy.

And no doubt she had been paid handsomely.

"They never would have connected anything to us if you hadn't dragged the whole thing out by trying to frame Ginger's stalker. It's not as if the sheriff's search warrant turned up anything."

Why did Reggie feel so comfortable saying all of this in front of her?

The next thought struck her hard. Because he doesn't intend for me to be able to repeat anything.

Her breath caught. She had to get out of here. She tried again to stand, but only made it to her knees before Cheryl's attention snapped toward her.

"She's trying to escape."

Reggie made no move to subdue Kaylee. "Here's the thing," he said to Cheryl in a terrifyingly calm voice. "Once people realize she's missing, you will be pegged as the last person she was seen with."

Cheryl blanched. "I didn't think of that."

"You never do."

"You've got to fix this."

Kaylee inched closer to the door, praying she'd have the strength to jump up and run for it once she was closer to it than they were.

"Don't worry. I will. I know if they arrest you, you'll crack and sell me out for the best deal they can offer, probably before they even get you into an interrogation room," he said snidely.

"I can't go to jail." Cheryl's voice cracked.

"So it has to appear to be self-defense. This florist followed you up here because she wants to make sure you're not going to sneak off before the sheriff catches up to you. Only solving the crime went to her head." He walked to the counter and snatched a butcher knife from the knife block. "When you brought her in here, she saw the knives and decided a good long one would help her escort you back down to the sheriff without any trouble."

Kaylee froze at the sight of him stalking toward Cheryl with the knife.

He jabbed it toward her chest.

Cheryl's arm swung up to block it, and the knife slashed her arm. "Ow! Are you crazy?"

"If you're going to claim self-defense, you need defensive wounds, don't you?"

Kaylee sprang to her feet and lurched toward the door.

Behind her, Reggie said, "You can't leave yet. We're not done." The knife clattered to the floor.

Her heart hammering in her ears, Kaylee yanked on the doorknob.

The door didn't budge.

Her fingers were still weak, and she lost her grip and tumbled to the floor.

Reggie loomed over her, wielding a heavy rolling pin. "Don't worry. Cheryl wouldn't retaliate against that nasty cut you gave her with a knife. She'll have to shock you again though."

Kaylee scurried away from him on all fours.

"And the police will be able to see she used it. And if the coroner is astute, he'll also conclude she tried to suffocate you while you were down. Just to knock you out, of course, so she could escape," Reggie went on.

"Why are you doing this?" Kaylee asked breathlessly, stalling for time. She prayed that by now, Reese would be wondering what was keeping them and would be racing through the school looking for her.

"You disappoint me. I thought you had it all figured out."

Kaylee swallowed hard. "Cheryl was spying for you and got scared her company had caught on and hired Amber to investigate. Cheryl probably thought Amber had snapped an incriminating photo of you two talking in the bush and panicked. So you killed Amber and stole her camera to make us think it was a robbery gone bad." Kaylee had managed to creep backward more than six feet, and he made no move to close the distance, so she went on talking, aiming for the second door in the extra-large room. "You also had to make sure Amber hadn't made any incriminating notes elsewhere, so you searched her room. Then you used her phone to remotely wipe her computer."

"Very good."

"And once you realized she'd taken the SD card out of her camera before you stole it, you had to make sure there were no photos on the card that could lead the police in your direction, so you stole Wilma's laptop from her car and hacked her e-mail to gain remote access to the computers of anyone who had e-mailed her photos."

He raised an eyebrow as if surprised she'd connected that little escapade to him as well.

"Did you text Arnold from her phone after he tried to call

her?" Kaylee studied his amused smile. "No, you're good, but it surely took you time to crack her password. I'm guessing she wrote it, and you got to her before she could relock it, which was how you could use it to wipe her hard drive."

"You have impressive skills of deduction. It's a shame you won't live long enough to share your conclusions with the authorities."

A chill ran up Kaylee's spine, but she suppressed the shiver. "Trust me, the sheriff knows," she boasted as nonchalantly as she could manage.

"About Cheryl, perhaps. But the fact you were more concerned about chasing after her and Phil than talking to me when you ran across the stage down there—even after learning from my wife that I left the hotel room Thursday night—tells me you only just put the puzzle pieces together."

"You can't get away with this. There's other evidence. You left shoe prints behind in Amber's hotel room and shards of glass from the crime scene. Shards still stuck in your shoe treads."

His eyes narrowed. "You're bluffing."

"No," Cheryl whispered. "They took impressions from Phil's shoes. They must've had something to compare them to."

The twitch in Reggie's cheek was his first hint of fear.

Kaylee decided that laying out the overwhelming amount of evidence might be her only hope of convincing him not to compound one murder charge with another, maybe give himself a chance of getting out on parole in twenty or thirty years. "The sheriff figured out you sabotaged my car tire after Cheryl spotted me studying the hotel's surveillance tapes."

Reggie shook his head. "That was all Cheryl."

"We also found an impression on the notepad she left behind in her hotel room of the note she left in Ginger's beach bag."

Reggie glared at Cheryl.

"Mr. Fletcher clued us in that Cheryl had been his best botany student, making it all the more surprising that she would get herself into hogweed. Well, surprising until the SD card from Amber's camera was found and we saw the picture of the two of you in the woods. I imagine plants were the last thing on her mind once she realized the PI she was so worried about had a rather suspicious photo of the two of you."

Cheryl's rash had faded considerably, but apparently the mere mention of it caused it to start itching because she squirmed and scratched it.

"Of course," Kaylee went on, "her botanical knowledge no doubt came in handy when she went hunting for poisonous mushrooms to take me out and when she spotted the convenient American bittersweet berries on the cruise's buffet table to once again make it seem as if Ginger's stalker had been behind everything. After all, he might have mistaken Amber's red hair for Ginger's and mistaken my SUV for Ginger's rental."

Reggie gritted his teeth and snarled at Cheryl, "You couldn't leave well enough alone, could you?" He swung the rolling pin in her direction and she screamed. "Shut up, woman. Do you want to be found out?"

Someone tried the door handle, then banged on the door. "Reggie, is that you? Let me in!" Nina called through the door.

Kaylee sprang to her feet and sprinted for the door she hadn't tried yet. "Help! Call the police." The rolling pin slammed into her back and sent her sprawling.

Reggie pressed a glove-covered hand over Kaylee's mouth.

Nina banged on the door again. "I know you're in there. Who's with you? I heard a woman's voice."

"Get over here and keep her quiet," Reggie hissed to Cheryl. When Cheryl obeyed, he went to the door and opened it a crack. "Nina, this is business. You need to go downstairs and forget what you heard. I'll be down shortly."

"But—"

Kaylee kicked and flailed and did her best to make as much noise as she could.

"No buts," Reggie said sternly. "If you say anything about this, we could be ruined. Now go. If anyone asks where I am, tell them I went outside to catch up with some of the guys."

Kaylee rammed her elbow into Cheryl's arm, breaking her grip on Kaylee's mouth. "He's going to kill you too," she whispered. "Can't you see? He wants it to look like I tried to subdue you and you fought back and we both died in the process."

Cheryl stopped fighting and stared at Reggie, who was closing the door on Nina.

He retrieved the knife.

"You heard him," Kaylee said. "The sheriff is after you. And Reggie doesn't trust you not to hang him out to dry."

Reggie pinned Kaylee with an icy sneer as he stepped closer with the knife.

"That's the knife he wants the sheriff to believe I attacked you with!" Kaylee screamed at Cheryl, who jumped at Kaylee's sudden outburst and let go of her. Kaylee scrambled to her feet and ran for the door. "You really think he intends to use it only on me? He needs us both dead." Kaylee yanked on the door, and it opened.

She didn't have time to be relieved. Reggie slammed the door against her, catching her body between the door and frame, then yanked her back inside, muffling her scream with his gloved hand.

She struggled against his hold, grabbing the doorknob to try to throw him off-balance.

He crowded her against the door, flattening her face against it. He suddenly screamed and convulsed wildly. His grip loosened, but not before Kaylee also felt the zap of Cheryl's stun gun.

Kaylee tore out of Reggie's weakening hold and snatched up the rolling pin.

The zap wasn't enough to take him down, but at least now Cheryl seemed to be fighting on Kaylee's side.

Reggie's gaze dropped to the knife lying on the floor.

Kaylee raced forward and kicked the knife across the room before he could reach it. "Cheryl didn't kill anyone!" she shouted at him, more for Cheryl's benefit than to rile him. "If she walks away now, she can cut a good deal for testifying against you."

He drew a gun. "If you think either of you will make it out of here alive, you're deluded."

20

Kaylee froze, gaping at Reggie's small pistol. Where had it come from?

"You shoot us with that, deputies will come running," Kaylee reasoned in a wobbly voice. "And no way will they believe we killed each other with a gun neither of us own. And if it's registered to you, you can forget about ever returning to your old life."

Reggie's sneer cut her off. "Shall I tell her? Or do you want to?" he asked Cheryl.

Cheryl peered at the gun, her face ashen. "No!" She dashed to her purse and dumped out the contents. "He's got my gun."

He chuckled. "That PI wasn't the only one with a talent for sleight-of-hand tricks."

Kaylee gauged the distance between herself and the door. Reggie was behind her. The path to freedom and safety was clear. Could she outrun a bullet?

Cheryl didn't have a chance now that Reggie stood between her and the door, but at least her position on the other side of him kept Reggie's attention divided. They could use that to their advantage.

"Here's the way I see this going down," Reggie said as if he were making plans for dinner instead of murder. "I'll hear gunshots, but I'll arrive too late to stop you from killing each other. Cheryl will whisper a confession with her dying breath, and I'll be frantically trying to revive one of you when the police arrive. That will be convincing, especially if one of you still has the gun. They'll assume there was a struggle, during which you shot each other." He glanced toward the knife, still on the floor where Kaylee had kicked it. "It's tricky with a shared gun, though.

Maybe Kaylee should use the knife."

Kaylee eyed the room's second door, the one that had been locked the first time she'd tried it, but that Reggie had since opened to speak to Nina. If Cheryl ran for it and Kaylee ran for the one closest to her, Reggie would have a harder time getting in two shots, which meant they had a better chance of one of them escaping to get help. And maybe he wasn't even a good shot. It wasn't his gun, after all.

"Have you ever even shot a gun?" Kaylee asked.

Reggie smirked. "I've been a gun club member since I was twenty. What do you think?"

Her heart dropped a beat. But she didn't see any other way out than running in opposite directions and hoping for the best. Only how did she tell Cheryl her plan without tipping off Reggie?

"You." Reggie pointed the gun at Cheryl and flicked it in Kaylee's direction. "Get over there with her."

"No!" Cheryl snatched a knife from the knife block and threw it at him. "Run!" she screamed.

The gun went off.

Kaylee yanked open the door and raced down the dark hall. "Help! Help!"

A shot took out the glass of the window next to her.

She reflexively ducked as she raced for the stairwell, screaming as loud as she could.

She heard Reese shout somewhere nearby. "Kaylee!"

"This way!" she screamed and veered into the stairwell. A third bullet ricocheted off the wall.

The corridor door below banged open.

"Up there!" a woman cried.

Dave rounded the first landing as Kaylee hit the top step.

Moving too quickly, Kaylee missed the second step and tumbled down to the landing. "Reggie killed Amber," she babbled as Reese reached her and pulled her to her feet. "And he's trying to kill me. I think he shot Cheryl."

Dave raced past them, a gun in his hand.

The outside door banged open and two deputies rushed in.

"Up there!" Kaylee pointed. "Reggie Blake has a gun and is trying to kill me. And the guy in the blue shirt with a gun is Ginger's bodyguard. He went up after Reggie."

One deputy ran up the stairs two at a time. The other went back outside and raced across to the door for the second wing, presumably to cut off any attempt to escape.

Reese helped her down the last of the steps. "Did he hurt you?"

"Cheryl zapped me with a stun gun and tried to suffocate me, but Reggie stopped her. He wanted to make it look as if we killed each other so no one would know his connection to everything." Kaylee swiped at the tears dripping down her face.

Reese's arm tightened. "I'm so sorry I didn't find you sooner. When you took so long to come back, I got to thinking about the text you sent me about the glass in Reggie's shoe treads. I raced all over the wrong wing trying to find you. I should have thought to—"

She shook her head. "It's over now." At least for her. She sent a quiet prayer heavenward for Cheryl not to be seriously injured, and for the deputies and Dave to bring Reggie down with no more bloodshed.

Nina hovered at the bottom of the stairwell. "I'm so sorry," she whispered to Kaylee. "I didn't know."

"You went for help?" Kaylee asked.

"I had to do something. I didn't know what Reggie was doing in there, but I heard someone scream for help. I couldn't have lived with myself if someone got hurt and I could have prevented it."

"Good for you," Reese said.

She hugged herself, but it didn't stop the tremors that had

overtaken her limbs. "I've been trying to ignore Reggie's illegal activities for too long because I love him. And I think sometimes he might have spiked my drinks and food so I'd forget what I'd seen or heard."

Kaylee shuddered at the thought of a husband doing that to his wife. It was a deep betrayal.

"I've decided I'm not playing by his rules anymore," Nina finished. "I'm glad you're safe."

Reese urged them all out of the confines of the stairwell into the safety of the auditorium, where the high school's principal and a couple of teachers had instituted a lockdown until the deputies issued an all clear.

Ginger hurried over to Kaylee as their little group made their way to some chairs. "Did you see Dave?"

"Yes, and he was fine when I saw him," Kaylee said.

"He went after Reggie with the deputies," Nina added.

Ewan joined them. "Reggie is Ginger's stalker?" His voice held surprise.

"No," Kaylee said tiredly, collapsing into a chair.

As if sensing the weariness in her bones, Reese forestalled further questions by saying, "The sheriff will want to be the first to hear her testimony."

Ewan nodded. "Of course." To Kaylee, he added, "I'm glad you're okay. You are okay, aren't you?"

"I'm fine. Thanks."

After what seemed like hours, but was probably not more than thirty minutes, the sheriff came in and spoke to the principal, then escorted Kaylee, Reese, and Nina to a more private area. "I've given instructions to allow everyone to leave in fifteen minutes through the front. My deputies have cordoned off the areas we've deemed part of the crime scene. I'll need all of you, especially you, Kaylee, to walk me through what happened here tonight."

"How is Cheryl?" Kaylee asked.

"She has a gunshot wound to the arm. She'll recover."

Kaylee breathed a relieved sigh. "Will the DA cut her a deal in exchange for flipping on Reggie?"

"I hope so. It'd make our case against him much easier to prosecute. But she won't be out of prison anytime soon with a corporate espionage charge on top of accessory to murder and attempted murder."

"She confessed to poisoning my water bottle?"

"No. That'd be another charge yet. Did she do it?"

"I honestly don't know which of them did it. But when I was stalling for time by trying to convince them you already knew what happened, I said Cheryl hunted up the mushrooms, and Reggie's reaction suggested I was right."

"Good to know. If she's smart, she'll cop to it in return for added leniency."

Kaylee rubbed the chill from her arms, not sure how she felt about giving the woman too many concessions. On the one hand, she'd probably saved Kaylee's life tonight. On the other, she'd endangered it multiple times this weekend. "Have your guys check Cheryl's purse and pockets and the cuffs of her sleeves. If she did it, you'll find mushroom spores."

Kaylee walked Eddie and Reese through a play-by-play of her entire ordeal from the moment she followed Cheryl upstairs. By the time she finished, she was utterly exhausted.

The sheriff took pity on her. "I think I have everything I need for now. Go home and get some rest."

Reese drove Kaylee home, occasionally glancing at her as if appraising her health for himself. "You're sure you're feeling all right? Maybe we should've had the paramedics check out the burns from the stun gun or at least check the oxygen level in your blood. How long did she hold that pillow over your face?"

"I'm fine," Kaylee replied. "It's only the adrenaline leaving my system."

When Reese pulled into her driveway, he said, "Can I make you a cup of tea before I go?"

"That would be nice. Thank you."

Bear greeted her exuberantly. She scooped him into her arms and carried him to the couch to cuddle him and let him soothe her residual jitters.

But she must've been more exhausted than she'd realized, because the next thing she knew, she woke on the couch to the sun slanting through the curtains. A cozy afghan was tucked around her, and Bear was watching her quietly.

"Thanks for letting me sleep, buddy. You ready to go out?"

She got up and took care of her dog, then showered. When she was dressed and feeling more like herself, she called Reese to thank him for taking such good care of her and to apologize for nodding off on him.

"I was happy to see you could sleep," he said. "Meet me for breakfast at Death by Chocolate?"

"I'd love to. Twenty minutes?"

"Perfect."

By the time Kaylee got into town, she could see through the bakery window that Reese already had a table for them. She quickly dropped off Bear inside The Flower Patch, then hurried next door.

As soon as she stepped inside Death by Chocolate, Jessica rushed around the counter and pulled Kaylee into a giant hug. "I'm so glad you're safe! I didn't hear about what happened until this morning or I would have come over to see you last night. It's all everyone's been talking about since I opened."

"I wasn't much company last night. I really just wanted to go to bed." Kaylee eased out of Jessica's embrace and glanced toward Reese to see that Wilma and Arnold had joined him.

Wilma sprang up and took Jessica's place giving Kaylee a hug. "I can't believe we missed all the excitement last night."

"You're fortunate. A lot of people weren't happy about being on lockdown for so long," Reese told her, waving to the empty seat beside him for Kaylee.

Wilma sank back down beside Arnold, who dropped his arm across her shoulders.

Jessica set an iced cappuccino in front of Kaylee. "On the house."

Kaylee grinned. "Thank you."

"Reggie." Arnold shook his head, sounding mystified. "I never would've believed it. Back in high school, the man was my idol. Now he's facing murder charges, two or three counts of attempted murder, and something about corporate espionage."

"I guess being popular and the best at everything you do isn't all it's cracked up to be, huh?" Kaylee said. "Reggie clearly didn't care who he hurt as long as he came out on top."

Arnold nodded. "You know what high school boys are like, though. Girls are all they have on the brain. So we can't help but envy any guy who can capture the interest of every good-looking girl in the school."

"True beauty is more than skin deep," Reese said.

"Well, this one has every kind of beauty," Arnold said, giving Wilma's shoulders a squeeze. "To think I wasted all those years being sure that if only I could be popular, that would be the best thing that could ever happen to me."

"And now?" Kaylee asked.

"Now I know there are more important things." He grinned. "Next week, I'm meeting with Dr. Byrne about taking over his dental practice here on the island when he retires next spring."

"You are?" Kaylee couldn't help but mirror Wilma's radiant grin.

"Yup," Arnold continued. "I've come to realize that being

popular pales in comparison to having the love of an amazing woman like Wilma."

Kaylee was surprised that they were already saying "love." Maybe it wasn't such a leap for them, though. After all, Wilma had adored Arnold for years.

"That deserves a toast." Reese lifted his coffee mug. "To many happy days ahead."

They all clinked mugs.

"And it looks like we may have another alum returning to Turtle Cove, at least part-time," Wilma said. "I heard Ginger made an offer on a summer house here. She and Dave are openly walking around hand in hand today, so it looks like they might be serious about each other."

Kaylee could not have been happier for either couple. "As my grandmother likes to say," Kaylee said, "happiness comes to those who stop coveting what others have and open their eyes to their own many blessings."

"A wise woman indeed." Arnold squeezed Wilma's hand, and Kaylee knew he finally appreciated everything he'd been given.

Kaylee glanced around the coffee shop, where friends were behind the counter and at almost every table. She thought of Bear, her family, her home, her business, and the new life she'd created for herself on this beautiful island.

She had more than a few blessings of her own.

Up to this point, we've been doing all the writing. Now it's *your* turn!

Tell us what you think about this book, the characters, the bad guy, or anything else you'd like to share with us about this series. We can't wait to hear from *you*!

Log on to give us your feedback at:
https://www.surveymonkey.com/r/FlowerShopMysteries

Annie's FICTION